The Palm-Wine Drinkard

Also by Amos Tutuola

Published by Grove Press

My Life in the Bush of Ghosts

AMOS TUTUOLA

The Palm-Wine Drinkard

and his dead Palm-Wine Tapster in the Dead's Town

With an Introduction
    by Michael Thelwell

GROVE PRESS, INC. • NEW YORK

First Black Cat Edition
First Printing 1984
ISBN: 0-394-62168-9
Library of Congress Catalog Card Number: 83-49449

Printed in the United States of America

GROVE PRESS, INC., 196 West Houston Street,
New York, N.Y. 10014

5   4   3

Introduction

It happened in the Yoruba town of Abeokuta, some-
what more than sixty but less than seventy years ago, on
a night just before the second Ogun festival. The sound
of singing and joyous cries rose from behind the tall mud
walls of the compound of the *Odafin* Odegbami. It was
the sound of the midwives praising the gods (*Orishas*)
and ancestors and proclaiming the birth of a boy.

The boy's father, the firstborn son of the *Odafin*, known
as *Tutuola*—"the gentle one"—received the news calmly
(this was not, after all, his first son). He uttered the traditional words of thanksgiving, rewarded the midwives,
and then made his way through the complex of rooms
and passageways to the *obi* or receiving room of his father where he informed the old man.

The *Odafin*, the spiritual leader of his clan, sub-chief,
and administrative ruler of a section of the city of Abeokuta, was a figure of power and authority, as befitted the
head of a large and influential compound. His name,
Odegbami, meant "Gift from Ogun," or alternately "It

was hunting that saved me" for the Yoruba language is subtle and flexible and the same combination of phrases can be variously interpreted. His strong name indicated that the *Odafin* was favored by the great *Orisha* Ogun, lord of fire and iron and therefore father of technology and political power and patron of smiths, warriors and hunters. He was "one of Ogun's children."

Anticipating his son's message, the old man would have had ready to hand kola and palm-wine with which to offer thanks and libation to the ancestors. Then he whispered into his son's ear the name already selected after divination and consultation with the elders. "His name shall be Olatubusun," the old man pronounced gravely. Tutuola thanked him for the name.

At sunrise the *Odafin* and his heir-apparent would go to offer the proper and necessary sacrifice of thanksgiving in the upper room where the great ancestral mask or *egugun* the visible symbol of the clan's power, resided. Then they would go to the *ile-Orisha*, the house of the *Orishas*, where the images of the gods were enshrined. But for the moment Tutuola took his leave and made his way back to the birth chamber where the grandmother waited to whisper the name and *irike* or birth-poem into the ear of the newborn, thus setting the new spirit in its appropriate place in the world of mankind, society, and history.

If Tutuola was disappointed at the name, he was not surprised. Looked at in one way, the name was almost a cliché. In its most obvious meaning Olatubusun could mean simply "wealth increases," which was, among the Yoruba and all African peoples, true of the birth of any child, particularly a son. He might have wished for a name more powerfully portentous, more resonant with omen. But a birth was not extraordinary in this household. The *Odafin* had six wives and more than twenty children and he himself had three wives and was already the father of a number of sons. Yet, like every father, he would have welcomed a name of unique power and promise, something that would mark even so junior a son for special prominence. Not that there was anything wrong with this name Olatubusun. For all wealth was not the same and no wealth was bad. The boy might be the bringer of a special kind of wealth, perhaps in ways not yet contemplated in the councils of the elders. For was not the world changing before their very eyes? Had not the great oracle under the rock foretold such change? By its very lack of specificity this name could suggest that the boy was specially chosen. This fourthborn son will see things that we have never seen, mused the gentle and thoughtful Tutuola as he went to look upon his son.

According to local legend a small band of refugees, fleeing the destruction of their town during a wave of slave-taking, were guided by a spirit to a cave in the side of a hill that was capped by a spectacular granite formation. There in the cave, "under the rock," or in Yoruba "Abeokuta," they found refuge. The cave became their most sacred shrine—the seat of an oracle—and the place where festivals of sacrifice and thanksgiving, ritual re-enactments of the salvation of the town's founders and the ongoing covenant with the protective spirit, were performed.

Secure in the covenant, the town prospered, and indeed, spread so widely that the king had to appoint surrogates for different sections of the city. These *Odafins*—an appointive rather than a hereditary position—were responsible under the authority of the king for the administration of local government, the collection of taxes, and the observance and enforcement of law and tradition, both religious and secular. To be effective these appointees would have had to be figures of recognized worth; men of substance, respect, probity, and virtue within the terms of the traditional values of the culture.

The fortunes and prominence of the family had reached its zenith with the appointment of the "father," Odegbami, as *Odafin* of their sector. Ironically, this rise in the family fortunes coincided with a serious erosion of the primacy of traditional values and practice. As befitted his civic status and influence, the *Odafin* had taken additional wives and expanded his compound. His son Tutuola, next in succession for head of the clan, did likewise. As was proper, the *Odafin* commissioned the finest artists of Abeokuta to create a new and elaborate *egugun*. This new ancestral mask, ornate and imposing in its awful beauty and authority, was consecrated and enshrined in an upper room specially built for that purpose. The elaborate mask was at once a symbol of the family's spiritual foundation and an expression of its material prosperity. So too was the *ile-ere* of the compound, the large room in which imposing images of important *Orishas—Shango, Oya, Ogun, Obatala—*were carefully tended and ministered to by the *Odafin* himself as part of his responsibility as spiritual head of the household. All of this was no more than what tradition required and was supported for a time by produce from ancestral lands and the revenues and entitlements of office.

What was not anticipated was the way in which the

integrity of the indigenous Yoruba institutions of Abeokuta would begin to feel an unprecedented and unassimilable pressure. This is not to say that the region had been culturally insulated. At the time of Odegbami's appointment (circa 1900–10), Islam had long been present and mosques were not unknown in the city. Islamic culture and doctrine and Yoruba belief and practice coexisted relatively free of tension for Islam in West Africa went back many centuries and each system had had time and pressing reason to adjust, however uneasily, to the peculiar character of the other.

The new pressure came at this time from an intolerant, bumptious, and vigorously proselytizing European Christianity, a new dispensation that was not to content itself with the harvesting of souls and the elevation of the spirit, but which increasingly set itself the task of transforming societies. The missionaries—courageous and mostly doomed—frequently brought, or possibly had to bring, to their civilizing mission that narrow self-righteousness that is so often the sword and shield of the religious idealist.

More significantly, hard on the heels of their chapels, mission schools, and hospitals had come new laws and moral codes which were enforced by native courts, a parallel civil service buttressed by police and military forces, a mercantile economy accompanied by a different system of currency, and a new and mysterious system of land tenure, all of which in combination represented during the transition first a parallel government and then a superceding one. The cumulative effect of this challenge on all the traditional institutions of religion, culture, education, commerce, and government was the growing devaluation of native conceptions of identity, authority, and value on civic, moral and personal levels alike.

It was during this period of transitional confusion—a chaos of values and moral authority—that the birth of Olatubusun was celebrated according to custom and tradition, in circumstances themselves emblematic of this tension.

The child was born into a powerfully traditional household—to Christian parents. From his earliest memories he recalls that "I met my father and mother as Christians." Though nearly all of his children adopted the new faith, the *Odafin* never did. While he lived, he was master of a traditional household in which all the *Orishas'* festivals were celebrated, ancestral feast days observed, and the spectacular dancing *egugun* regularly received the petitions and offerings of women wanting children. Every Thursday the household awakened to the sound of ritual drumming and the chanting of the *babalawo* or sacred drummer. On Sundays the Christians went to church. But in that house, young Olatubusun remembers, "in a large room I met all the gods, Ogun, god of iron, Shango, god of thunder, Oya, Oshun, Obatala . . . all of them." This was an encounter certain to make a lasting impression on the young boy. As Robert Farris Thompson, our most inspired Africanist, has observed, "A child growing up among the Yoruba is exposed daily to one of the finest traditions of sculpture produced by any people." And the pantheon of gods, the *Orisha* system, was considered by Frobenious to be "richer, more original, more rigorous, and well-preserved than any of the forms coming down to us from classical antiquity."

But the youthful imagination was fed not only by the

awesome images looming in the dim, sacred *ile-ere*. Ritual, spectacle, song, dance, drumbeats, mystery, and power surrounded him. Poetry, pageantry, and history combined in the luminous presence of the *egugun* as the ancestor became flesh and danced among his children. The boy was attracted to the art of the storyteller, a tradition of oral literature that had reached a very high level of complexity and diversity among the Yoruba. But to call these expressions of the culture "stories" is reductive. As developed in this culture, their elaborate narrative line incorporated elements of theater, music, mime, ritual, magic, dance, and the linguistic elements of proverb, poetry, riddle, parable, and song. They were not told so much as performed, dramatically re-enacted, so that the accomplished taleteller had to be master of a range of skills. He was at once actor, mime, impressionist, singer, dancer, composer, and conductor, using his range of artistic skills and even the audience and environment to create a multidimensional experience that has no obvious equivalent in Western culture. A more elaborate expression of this form—most often with a strictly religious reference, being ritual recreations of sacred myths—was performed by costumed dancers to the accompaniment of religious music, and became known to Western observers as "folk operas."

It was in this dynamic, powerfully dramatic, and evocative, yet extremely *ordered* environment that the boy's formative sensibilities developed. At about fourteen years old, a new Christian, he left the traditional compound for the Salvation Army School, literally a new world. The death of the distinguished grandfather, followed a few years later by that of the father, brought further changes. The family yielded to new realities and Europeanized their name. Mostly in deference to the great man—now a respected ancestor—who had brought them prominence, they took the surname *Odegbami*. Only the boy Olatubusun, junior though he was in the lineage, dissented. He either chose or was given the Christian name Amos for the fierce old prophet of righteousness ("Justice shall come down like a mighty water. . . ."). And with filial loyalty he took his father's name, hence Amos Tutuola.

Change was rapid. The grand household of the *Odafin* could not be maintained. In this transition period, there appear to have been the usual problems of succession, inheritance, entitlement, and questions about which lands belonged to the family (who in any case had now neither the power, prestige, or revenues of former times) and which to the office. The family dispersed to make their way in the strange world where 2,000 cowries, a substantial sum in traditional exchange, translated to sixpence in British currency. Amos Tutuola attended the Anglican Central School in Abeokuta while his father, now living on some family lands a short distance from Abeokuta, was alive. Upon his death the "junior" son had to end his formal education. He went to Lagos, became apprenticed to a coppersmith, and joined the British army, occupations that must have brought a smile to the face of the dead grandfather since both were under the jurisdiction of his patron, *Orisha*, Ogun.

At the war's end he was demobilized with thousands of other young men and thrust upon his own devices to make his way in the world. He secured, in his own words, "this unsatisfactory job" as a messenger in one of the civil service departments in Lagos. There he might have lived and worked in modest circumstances and obscurity save for a fortuitous accident. One of the Commonwealth information journals that the British used to circulate in their colonial territori s and at home caught the eye of Mr. Tutuola. His attention was attracted to the cover, an impressive full-color reproduction of a sculpture of an *Orisha*. The section on Nigeria contained many such "portraits" of gods, artfully photographed in ᵒlor, and his mind rushed back to the *ile-ere* of his grandfather's compound. He bought the journal.

Well, it happened that since I was young and I was in the infant school which we call nowadays primary, each time I went to my village I learnt many tales and I was much interested in it so that later when I could read and write I wrote many of them down. And as much as I had great interest in these, I took myself to be one of the best taletellers in the school for the other children. Later, having left the school, one day I bought one magazine. I was working then. I had joined the army and left the army. I was engaged as a messenger by the Department of Labor. One day I got one magazine published by the Government of Nigeria Information Service. It carried all the festivals, Oya, Ogun everything. It was a quarterly magazine, so I bought the magazine and started to read it. It contained very lovely portraits of the gods. When I bought the magazine I read it to a page where books which were published were advertised. Well . . . I had read some of those books when I was at school. Then I saw that one of the books which were advertised here was about our tales, our Yoruba tales. "But Eh! By the way, when I was at school I was a good taleteller! Why, could I not write my own? Ooh, I am very good at this thing." The following day I took up my pen and paper and I started to write The Palm-Wine Drinkard. *Well, I wrote the script of* Palm-*

Wine *and kept it in the house. I didn't know where to send it to.*

Again, the following quarter I bought another magazine of the same type. Fortunately when I read it, I got to where it advertised "Manuscripts Wanted" overseas. Well then! Immediately I sent my story to the advertiser. When my script got to them they wrote me in about two weeks saying that they did not accept manuscripts which were not concerned with religion, Christian religion. But, they would not return my manuscript. They would find a publisher for me because the story was so strange to them that they would not be happy if they returned it to me. By that I should be patient with them to help me find a publisher. Then a year later I got a letter from Faber & Faber that they got my manuscript from Lutheran World Press. Faber & Faber said that the story . . . uh they were wondering whether I found the story fallen down from somebody because it is very strange to them. They wondered because they were surprised to see such a story . . . they wanted to know whether I had made it up or got it from somebody else . . . and they would be happy if I would leave the story for them to do it as they want. I reply that I didn't know anything about book publishing and so on, so I leave everything for you to do as you see is good. . . . Then after about six months now they publish the book in 1952 and sent a copy to me. That is how I started to write.

What was in my mind? Well. Oh . . . the time I wrote it, what was in my mind was that I noticed that our young men, our young sons and daughters did not pay much attention to our traditional things or culture or customs. They adopted, they concentrated their minds only on European things. They left our customs, so if I do this they may change their mind . . . to remember our custom, not to leave it to die. . . . That was my intention."

Appearing unannounced and without fanfare in the British edition in 1952 and in the Grove Press American edition in 1953, the book has had the kind of career of which publishing legends are made. I cannot say to what extent the lineage's "wealth increased" as a consequence, but certainly the book has continued in print ever since. It has been translated into fifteen languages, European and non-European as well. It seems to enjoy a respectable and steady circulation and to have attracted a loyal following worldwide. It is frequently to be found on syllabi of university courses in religion, anthropology, psychology, and even literature and has been followed by *My Life in the Bush of Ghosts* (1954) and *The Brave African Huntress*.

I shall not speculate—intriguing though that prospect be—on precisely which chords of modern literary sensibility are set resonating under the stimulus of *Drinkard*'s unique vision. Certainly one can see where certain Jungian and Freudian critics could, with barely compatible assumptions, find much to engage them in its world. So too can surrealists and devotees of magical realism find within its hospitable territory on which to plant their respective standards. It is, however, more important to attempt to identify the cultural and intellectual provenance of the material, and to determine its specific relationship to the traditions that produced it.

This novel is a cultural hybrid, the child of the clash of cultures I have been describing. The stories in it are translations—more accurately, transliterations—of conventional folktales into the idiomatic "young English", as Dylan Thomas called it, of the Nigerian masses. It is clear from the reading, and even more so when one listens to the author telling a story, exactly how difficult the translation process really is. This is not simply "young English" but *new* English, an English whose vocabulary is bent and twisted into the service of a different language's nuances, syntax, and interior logic. The result is original and often startling.

Apart from the aesthetic distance between rhetorical devices, linguistic traditions, rhythms, puns, repetitions, cadences, nuances, metaphors, and idioms, the total poetic sensibility of one language and culture and that of another, there is a further consideration. We are looking at only one element of the form. The other inclusive aesthetic dimensions of the tradition—dramatic voice, expression, pantomime, song, and rhythm are necessarily absent in the purely literary form. To that extent it is a new form. And if the form is new, what survives presumably must be "sensibility."

It is usual to hear that these tales express the "traditional sensibility" of an "African" world view and offer a window into the inchoate and frightening world of the primitive imagination. So general a statement would be quite misleading. The stories and the narrative and visionary techniques reflect one particular and identifiable aspect of a complex and sophisticated tradition.

The central Yoruba tradition—that of the sacred myth describing the creation, evolution, and jurisdiction of the deities and historical heroes—represents a remarkably rigorous cosmology of intellectual coherence and elegance. It is a universe of elemental forces both natural and social which finds metaphoric expression in a pantheon of deities, whose complicated interrelationships, jurisdictions, and necessities are rationalized into an architectonic system of knowledge. The sophisticated world view embodied in this myth has as its central value the balancing and harmonizing of powerful forces—natural, numinous, and social.

Out of the interplay of deities, ancestors, and humanity, through a process of mutual obligation expressed in language, ritual, and protocol as handed down by tradition, society became possible. A universe of history, stability, morality, and order was achieved.

But bordering on this system of stability was terra incognito: the evil forest, the bad bush. Here was the home of chaos, where random spirits without name or history, of bizarre forms and malignant intent were to be found. This was the domain of the deformed, the unnatural, and the abominable. The Sunufo, distant cousins of the Yoruba, have a mask that expresses this. It has the snout of an alligator, the tusk of a boar, the horn of a rhinoceros, and the ears of a zebra. It represents an animal that existed before order was imposed on the world.

In the oral tradition the folktale—a moral and cautionary story but clearly recognized as fiction and entertainment—had free range of this random and arbitrary world. Because they were intended for entertainment and instruction, these tales could be as horrific, frightening, and bizarre as the imagination could render them They required the willing suspension of disbelief.

Many of Tutuola's motifs and even complete tales an images are drawn from this genre. But the structure and cumulative effect, the vision, is the creation of this sensitive and pensive man. To what extent this overriding vision, one of constant suffering, danger, insecurity, and struggle is the product of the cultural trauma, uncertainty, and psychic alienation through which that generation passed is hard to say.

Amos Tutuola says that he wrote to "tell of my ancestors and how they lived in their days. They lived with immortal creatures of the forest. But now the forests are gone. I believe the immortal creatures must have moved away."

Some years ago he returned to the ancestral compound in order to visit the *ile-Orisha*. The compound was ruinate, the *egugun* had disappeared, and in his words, "The gods had perished."

—Michael Thelwell
April, 1984

I was a palm-wine drinkard since I was a boy of ten years of age. I had no other work more than to drink palm-wine in my life. In those days we did not know other money, except COWRIES, so that everything was very cheap, and my father was the richest man in our town.

My father got eight children and I was the eldest among them, all of the rest were hard workers, but I myself was an expert palm-wine drinkard. I was drinking palm-wine from morning till night and from night till morning. By that time I could not drink ordinary water at all except palm-wine.

But when my father noticed that I could not do any work more than to drink, he engaged an expert palm-wine tapster for me; he had no other work more than to tap palm-wine every day.

So my father gave me a palm-tree farm which was nine miles square and it contained 560,000 palm-trees, and this palm-wine tapster was tapping one hundred and fifty kegs of palm-wine every morning, but before 2 o'clock p.m., I would have drunk all of it; after that he would go and tap another 75 kegs in the evening which I would be drinking till morning. So my friends were uncountable by that time and they were drinking palm-wine with me from morning till a late hour in the night. But when my palm-wine tapster completed the period of 15 years that he was tapping the palm-wine for me, then my father died suddenly, and when it was the 6th month after my father had died, the tapster went to the palm-tree farm on a Sunday evening to tap palm-wine for me. When he reached the farm, he climbed one of the tallest palm-trees in the farm to tap palm-wine but as he was tapping on, he fell down unexpectedly and died at the foot of the palm-tree as a result of injuries. As I was waiting for him to bring the palm-wine, when I saw that he did not return in time, because he was not keeping me long like that before, then I called two of my friends to accompany me to the farm. When we reached the farm, we began to look at every palm-tree, after a while we found him under the palm-tree, where he fell down and died.

But what I did first when we saw him dead there, was that I climbed another palm-tree which was near the spot, after that I tapped palm-wine and drank it to my satisfaction before I came back to the spot. Then both my friends who accompanied me to the farm and I dug a pit under the palm-tree that he fell down as a grave and buried him there, after that we came back to the town.

When it was early in the morning of the next day, I had no palm-wine to drink at all, and throughout that day I felt not so happy as before; I was seriously sat down in my parlour, but when it was the third day that I had no palm-wine at all, all my friends did not come to my house again, they left me there alone, because there was no palm-wine for them to drink.

But when I completed a week in my house without palm-wine, then I went out and, I saw one of them in

8

the town, so I saluted him, he answered but he did not approach me at all, he hastily went away.

Then I started to find out another expert palm-wine tapster, but I could not get me one who could tap the palm-wine to my requirement. When there was no palm-wine for me to drink I started to drink ordinary water which I was unable to taste before, but I did not satisfy with it as palm-wine.

When I saw that there was no palm-wine for me again, and nobody could tap it for me, then I thought within myself that old people were saying that the whole people who had died in this world, did not go to heaven directly, but they were living in one place somewhere in this world. So that I said that I would find out where my palm-wine tapster who had died was.

One fine morning, I took all my native juju and also my father's juju with me and I left my father's home-town to find out whereabouts was my tapster who had died.

But in those days, there were many wild animals and every place was covered by thick bushes and forests; again, towns and villages were not near each other as nowadays, and as I was travelling from bushes to bushes and from forests to forests and sleeping inside it for many days and months, I was sleeping on the branches of trees, because spirits etc. were just like partners, and to save my life from them; and again I could spend two or three months before reaching a town or a village. Whenever I reached a town or a village, I would spend almost four months there, to find out my palm-wine tapster from the inhabitants of that town or village and if he did not

9

reach there, then I would leave there and continue my journey to another town or village. After the seventh month that I had left my home town, I reached a town and went to an old man, this old man was not a really man, he was a god and he was eating with his wife when I reached there. When I entered the house I saluted both of them, they answered me well, although nobody should enter his house like that as he was a god, but I myself was a god and juju-man. Then I told the old man (god) that I am looking for my palm-wine tapster who had died in my town some time ago, he did not answer to my question but asked me first what was my name? I replied that my name was "Father of gods" who could do everything in this world, then he said: "was that true" and I said yes; after that he told me to go to his native black-smith in an unknown place, or who was living in another town, and bring the right thing that he had told the black-smith to make for him. He said that if I could bring the right thing that he told the black-smith to make for him, then he would believe that I was the "Father of gods who could do everything in this world" and he would tell me where my tapster was.

Immediately this old man told or promised me so, I went away, but after I had travelled about one mile away then I used one of my juju and at once I changed into a very big bird and flew back to the roof of the old man's house; but as I stood on the roof of his house, many people saw me there. They came nearer and looked at me on the roof, so when the old man noticed that many had surrounded his house and were looking at the roof, he and his wife came out from the house and when

10

he saw me (bird) on the roof, he told his wife that if he had not sent me to his native black-smith to bring the bell that he told the black-smith to make for him, he would tell me to mention the name of the bird. But at the same time that he said so, I knew what he wanted from the black-smith and I flew away to his black-smith, then when I reached there I told the black-smith that the old man (god) told me to bring his bell which he had told him to make for him. So the black-smith gave me the bell; after that, I returned to the old man with the bell and when he saw me with the bell, he and his wife were surprised and also shocked at that moment.

After that he told his wife to give me food, but after I had eaten the food, he told me again, that there remained another wonderful work to do for him, before he would tell me whereabouts my tapster was. When it was 6.30 a.m. of the following morning, he (god) woke me up, and gave me a wide and strong net which was the same in colour as the ground of that town. He told me to go and bring "Death" from his house with the net. When I left his house or the town about a mile, there I saw a junction of roads and I was doubtful when I reached the junction, I did not know which was Death's road among these roads, and when I thought within myself that as it was the market day, and all the market goers would soon be returning from the market—I lied down on the middle of the roads, I put my head to one of the roads, my left hand to one, right hand to another one, and my both feet to the rest, after that I pretended as I had slept there. But when all the market goers were returning from the market, they saw me lied down there and shouted thus:—"Who was the mother of this fine boy, he slept on the roads and put his head towards Death's road."

Then I began to travel on Death's road, and I spent about eight hours to reach there, but to my surprise I did not meet anybody on this road until I reached there and I was afraid because of that. When I reached his (Death's) house, he was not at home by that time, he was in his yam garden which was very close to his house, and I met a small rolling drum in his verandah, then I beat it to Death as a sign of salutation. But when he (Death) heard the sound of the drum, he said thus:— "Is that man still alive or dead?" Then I replied "I am still alive and I am not a dead man."

But at the same time that he heard so from me, he was greatly annoyed and he commanded the drum with a kind of voice that the strings of the drum should tight me there; as a matter of fact, the strings of the drum tighted me so that I was hardly breathing.

When I felt that these strings did not allow me to breathe and again every part of my body was bleeding too much, then I myself commanded the ropes of the yams in his garden to tight him there, and the yams in his garden to tight him there, and the yam stakes should begin to beat him also. After I had said so and at the same time, all the ropes of the yams in his garden tighted him hardly, and all the yam stakes were beating him repeatedly, so when he (Death) saw that these stakes were beating him repeatedly, then he commanded the strings of the drum which tighted me to release me, and I was released at the same time. But when I saw that I was released, then I myself commanded the ropes of the yams to release him and the yam stakes to stop beating him, and he was released at once. After he was released by the ropes of yams and yam stakes, he came to his house and met me at his verandah, then we shook hands together, and he told me to enter the house, he put me to one of his rooms, and after a while, he brought food to me and we ate it together, after that we started conversations which went thus:—He (Death) asked me from where did I come? I replied that I came from a certain town which was not so far from his place. Then he asked what did I come to do? I told him that I had been hearing about him in my town and all over the world and I thought within myself that one day I should come and visit or to know him personally. After that he replied that his work was only to kill the people of the world, after that he got up and told me to follow him and I did so.

He took me around his house and his yam garden too, he showed me the skeleton bones of human-beings which he had killed since a century ago and showed me many other things also, but there I saw that he was using skeleton bones of human-beings as fuel woods and skull heads of human-beings as his basins, plates and tumblers etc.

Nobody was living near or with him there, he was living lonely, even bush animals and 'birds were very far away from his house. So when I wanted to sleep at night, he gave me a wide black cover cloth and then gave me a separate room to sleep inside, but when I entered the room, I met a bed which was made with bones of human-beings; but as this bed was terrible to look at or to sleep on it, I slept under it instead, because I knew his trick already. Even as this bed was very terrible, I was unable to sleep under as I lied down there because of fear of the bones of human-beings, but I lied down there awoke. To my surprise was that when it was about two o'clock in the mid-night, there I saw somebody enter into the room cautiously with a heavy club in his hands, he came nearer to the bed on which he had told me to sleep, then he clubbed the bed with all his power, he clubbed the centre of the bed thrice and he returned cautiously, he thought that I slept on that bed and he thought also that he had killed me.

But when it was 6 o'clock early in the morning, I first woke up and went to the room in which he slept, I woke him up, so when he heard my voice, he was frightened, even he could not salute me at all when he got up from his bed, because he thought that he had killed me last night.

But the second day that I slept there, he did not attempt to do anything again, but I woke up by two o'clock of that night, and went to the road which I should follow to the town and I travelled about a quarter of a mile to his house, then I stopped and dug a pit of his (Death's) size on the centre of that road, after that I spread the net which the old man gave me to bring him (Death) with on that pit, then I returned to his house, but he did not wake up as I was playing this trick.

When it was 6 o'clock in the morning, I went to his door and woke him up as usual, then I told him that I wanted to return to my town this morning, so that I

14

wanted him to lead me a short distance; then he got up from his bed and he began to lead me as I told him, but when he led me to the place that I had dug, I told him to sit down, so I myself sat down on the road side, but as he sat down on the net, he fell into the pit, and without any ado I rolled up the net with him and put him on my head and I kept going to the old man's house who told me to go and bring him Death.

As I was carrying him along the road, he was trying all his efforts to escape or to kill me, but I did not give him a chance to do that. When I had travelled about eight hours, then I reached the town and went straight to the old man's house who told me to go and bring Death from his house. When I reached the old man's house, he was inside his room, then I called him and told him that I had brought Death that he told me to go and bring. But immediately he heard from me that I had brought Death and when he saw him on my head, he was greatly terrified and raised alarm that he thought nobody could go and bring Death from his house, then he told me to carry him (Death) back to his house at once, and he (old man) hastily went back to his room and started to close all his doors and windows, but before he could close two or three of his windows, I threw down Death before his door and at the same time that I threw him down, the net cut into pieces and Death found his way out.

Then the old man and his wife escaped through the windows and also the whole people in that town ran away for their lives and left their properties there. (The old man had thought that Death would kill me if I went to his house, because nobody could reach Death's

15

house and return, but I had known the old man's trick already.)

So that since the day that I had brought Death out from his house, he has no permanent place to dwell or stay, and we are hearing his name about in the world. This was how I brought out Death to the old man who told me to go and bring him before he (old man) would tell me whereabouts my palm-wine tapster was that I was looking for before I reached that town and w t to the old man.

But the old man who had promised me that if I could go to Death's house and bring him, he would tell me whereabouts my palm-wine tapster was, could not wait and fulfil his promise because he himself and his wife were narrowly escaped from that town.

Then I left the town without knowing where my tapster was, and I started another fresh journey.

When it was the fifth month since I had left that town, then I reached another town which was not so big, although there was a large and famous market. At the same time that I entered the town, I went to the house of the head of the town who received me with kindness into his house; after a little while he told one of his wives to give me food and after I had eaten the food, he told his wife to give me palm-wine too; I drank the palm-wine to excess as when I was in my town or as when my tapster was alive. But when I tasted the palm-wine given to me there, I said that I got what I wanted here. After I had eaten the food and drunk the palm-wine to my satisfaction, the head of the town who received me as his guest asked for my name, I told him that my name was

16

called "Father of gods who could do anything in this world." As he heard this from me, he was soon faint with fear. After that he asked me what I came to him for. I replied that I was looking for my palm-wine tapster who had died in my town some time ago. Then he told me that he knew where the tapster was.

After that he told me that if I could help him to find out his daughter who was captured by a curious creature from the market which was in that town, and bring her to him, then he would tell me whereabouts my tapster was.

He said furthermore that as I called myself "Father of gods who could do anything in this world," this would be very easy for me to do; he said so.

I did not know that his daughter was taken away by a curious creature from the market

I was about to refuse to go and find out his daughter who was taken away from the market by a curious creature, but when I remembered my name I was ashamed to refuse. So I agreed to find out his daughter. There was a big market in this town from where the daughter was captured, and the market-day was fixed for every 5th day and the whole people of that town and from all the villages around the town and also spirits and curious creatures from various bushes and forests were coming to this market every 5th day to sell or buy articles. By 4 o'clock in the evening, the market would close for that day and then everybody would be returning to his or her destination or to where he or she came from. But the daughter of the head of that town was a petty trader and she was due to be married before she was taken away from the market. Before that time, her father was

17

telling her to marry a man but she did not listen to her father; when her father saw that she did not care to marry anybody, he gave her to a man for himself, but this lady refused totally to marry that man who was introduced to her by her father. So that her father left her to herself.

This lady was very beautiful as an angel but no man could convince her for marriage. So, one day she went to the market on a market-day as she was doing before, or to sell her articles as usual; on that market-day, she saw a curious creature in the market, but she did not know where the man came from and never knew him before.

THE DESCRIPTION OF THE
CURIOUS CREATURE:—

He was a beautiful "complete" gentleman, he dressed with the finest and most costly clothes, all the parts of his body were completed, he was a tall man but stout. As this gentleman came to the market on that day, if he had been an article or animal for sale, he would be sold at least for £2000 (two thousand pounds). As this complete gentleman came to the market on that day, and at the same time that this lady saw him in the market, she did nothing more than to ask him where he was living, but this fine gentleman did not answer her or approach her at all. But when she noticed that the fine or complete gentleman did not listen to her, she left her articles and began to watch the movements of the complete gentleman about in the market and left her articles unsold.

By and by the market closed for that day then the whole people in the market were returning to their destinations etc., and the complete gentleman was returning to his own too, but as this lady was following him about in the market all the while, she saw him when he was returning to his destination as others did, then she was following him (complete gentleman) to an unknown place. But as she was following the complete gentleman along the road, he was telling her to go back or not to follow him, but the lady did not listen to what he was telling her, and when the complete gentleman had tired of telling her not to follow him or to go back to her town, he left her to follow him.

"DO NOT FOLLOW UNKNOWN MAN'S BEAUTY"

But when they had travelled about twelve miles away from that market, they left the road on which they were travelling and started to travel inside an endless forest in which only all the terrible creatures were living.

"RETURN THE PARTS OF BODY TO THE OWNERS; OR HIRED PARTS OF THE COMPLETE GENTLEMAN'S BODY TO BE RETURNED"

As they were travelling along in this endless forest then the complete gentleman in the market that the

lady was following, began to return the hired parts of
his body to the owners and he was paying them the
rentage money. When he reached where he hired the
left foot, he pulled it out, he gave it to the owner and
paid him, and they kept going; when they reached the
place where he hired the right foot, he pulled it out and
gave it to the owner and paid for the rentage. Now
both feet had returned to the owners, so he began to
crawl along on the ground, by that time, that lady wanted
to go back to her town or her father, but the terrible
and curious creature or the complete gentleman did not
allow her to return or go back to her town or her father
again and the complete gentleman said thus:— "I had
told you not to follow me before we branched into this
endless forest which belongs to only terrible and curious
creatures, but when I became a half-bodied incomplete
gentleman you wanted to go back, now that cannot be
done, you have failed. Even you have never seen anything yet, just follow me."

When they went furthermore, then they reached
where he hired the belly, ribs, chest etc., then he pulled
them out and gave them to the owner and paid for the
rentage.

Now to this gentleman or terrible creature remained
only the head and both arms with neck, by that time he
could not crawl as before but only went jumping on as
a bull-frog and now this lady was soon faint for this fearful creature whom she was following. But when the
lady saw every part of this complete gentleman in the
market was spared or hired and he was returning them
to the owners, then she began to try all her efforts to

return to her father's town, but she was not allowed by this fearful creature at all.

When they reached where he hired both arms, he pulled them out and gave them to the owner, he paid for them; and they were still going on in this endless forest, they reached the place where he hired the neck, he pulled it out and gave it to the owner and paid for it as well.

"A FULL-BODIED GENTLEMAN REDUCED TO HEAD"

Now this complete gentleman was reduced to head and when they reached where he hired the skin and flesh which covered the head, he returned them, and paid to the owner, now the complete gentleman in the market reduced to a "SKULL" and this lady remained with only "Skull". When the lady saw that she remained with only Skull, she began to say that her father had been telling her to marry a man, but she did not listen to or believe him.

When the lady saw that the gentleman became a Skull, she began to faint, but the Skull told her if she would die she would die and she would follow him to his house. But by the time that he was saying so, he was humming with a terrible voice and also grew very wild and even if there was a person two miles away he would not have to listen before hearing him, so this lady began to run away in that forest for her life, but the Skull chased her and within a few yards, he caught her, because he was very clever and smart as he was only

Skull and he could jump a mile to the second before coming down. He caught the lady in this way: so when the lady was running away for her life, he hastily ran to her front and stopped her as a log of wood.

By and by, this lady followed the Skull to his house, and the house was a hole which was under the ground. When they reached there both of them entered the hole. But there were only Skulls living in that hole. At the same time that they entered the hole, he tied a single Cowrie on the neck of this lady with a kind of rope, after that, he gave her a large frog on which she sat as a stool, then he gave a whistle to a Skull of his kind to keep watch on this lady whenever she wanted to run away. Because the Skull knew already that the lady would attempt to run away from the hole. Then he went to the back-yard to where his family were staying in the day time till night.

But one day, the lady attempted to escape from the hole, and at the same time that the Skull who was watching her whistled to the rest of the Skulls that were in the back-yard, the whole of them rushed out to the place where the lady sat on the bull-frog, so they caught her, but as all of them were rushing out, they were rolling on the ground as if a thousand petrol drums were pushing along a hard road. After she was caught, then they brought her back to sit on the same frog as usual. If the Skull who was watching her fell asleep, and if the lady wanted to escape, the cowrie that was tied on her neck would raise up the alarm with a terrible noise, so that the Skull who was watching her would wake up at once and then the rest of the Skull's family would rush out from the back in thousands to the lady and ask her what she wanted to do with a curious and terrible voice.

But the lady could not talk at all, because as the cowrie had been tied on her neck, she became dumb at the same moment.

THE FATHER OF GODS SHOULD FIND OUT WHEREABOUTS THE DAUGHTER OF THE HEAD OF THE TOWN WAS

Now as the father of the lady first asked for my name and I told him that my name was "Father of gods who could do anything in this world," then he told me that if I could find out where his daughter was and bring her to him, then he would tell me where my palm-wine tapster was. But when he said so, I was jumping up with gladness that he should promise me that he would tell me where my tapster was. I agreed to what he said; the father and parent of this lady never knew whereabouts their daughter was, but they had information that the lady followed a complete gentleman in the market. As I was the "Father of gods who could do anything in this world," when it was at night I sacrificed to my juju with a goat.

And when it was early in the morning, I sent for forty kegs of palm-wine, after I had drunk it all, I started to investigate whereabouts was the lady. As it was the market-day, I started the investigation from the market. But as I was a juju-man, I knew all the kinds of people in that market. When it was exactly 9 o'clock a.m., the very complete gentleman whom the lady followed

And when it was early in the morning, I sent for foarty kegs of palm-wine, after I had drunk it all, then I started to investigate where about the lady. As it was the market day, I started the investigation from the market. But as I was a jujuman, I knew all the kind of people in that market. When it was exactly 9 o'clock a.m., the very complete gentleman whom the lady followed came to the market again, and at the same time that I saw him, I knew that he was a curious and terrible creature.

*THE LADY WAS NOT TO BE BLAMED FOR FOLLOWING THE SKULL AS A COMPLETE GENTLEMAN!'

I could not blame the lady for following the skull as a complete gentleman to his house.
Because if I were a lady, no doubt I would follow him to where-ever he would go, and still as I was a man I would jealous him more than that, because if this gentleman to the battle field, surely, enemy would not kill him or capture him and if bombers see him in a town which was to be bombed, they would not throw bombs on his presence, and if they throw it, the bomb itself would not explode until this gentleman would leave that town, because of his beauty. At the same time that I saw this gentleman in the market on that day, what I was doing was only to follow him about in the market. After I looked at him for so many hours, then I ran to a corner of the market and I cried for a few minutes, because I thought within myself I was not created with beauty as this gentleman, but when I remembered that he was only a —

A page from the author's MS. showing the publisher's 'corrections' came to the market again, and at the same time that I saw him, I knew that he was a curious and terrible creature.

"THE LADY WAS NOT TO BE BLAMED FOR FOLLOWING THE SKULL AS A COMPLETE GENTLEMAN"

I could not blame the lady for following the Skull as a complete gentleman to his house at all. Because if I were a lady, no doubt I would follow him to wherever he would go, and still as I was a man I would jealous him more than that, because if this gentleman went to the battle field, surely, enemy would not kill him or capture him and if bombers saw him in a town which was to be bombed, they would not throw bombs on his presence, and if they did throw it, the bomb itself would not explode until this gentleman would leave that town, because of his beauty. At the same time that I saw this gentleman in the market on that day, what I was doing was only to follow him about in the market. After I looked at him for so many hours, then I ran to a corner of the market and I cried for a few minutes because I thought within myself why was I not created with beauty as this gentleman, but when I remembered that he was only a Skull, then I thanked God that He had created me without beauty, so I went back to him in the market, but I was still attracted by his beauty. So when the market closed for that day, and when everybody was returning to his or her destination, this gentleman was returning to his own too and I followed him to know where he was living.

"INVESTIGATION TO THE SKULL'S FAMILY'S HOUSE"

When I travelled with him a distance of about twelve miles away to that market, the gentleman left the really road on which we were travelling and branched into an endless forest and I was following him, but as I did not want him to see that I was following him, then I used one of my juju which changed me into a lizard and followed him. But after I had travelled with him a distance of about twenty-five miles away in this endless forest, he began to pull out all the parts of his body and return them to the owners, and paid them.

After I had travelled with him for another fifty miles in this forest, then he reached his house and entered it, but I entered it also with him, as I was a lizard. The first thing that he did when he entered the hole (house) he went straight to the place where the lady was, and I saw the lady sat on a bull-frog with a single cowrie tied on her neck and a Skull who was watching her stood behind her. After he (gentleman) had seen that the lady was there, he went to the back-yard where all his family were working.

"THE INVESTIGATOR'S WONDERFUL WORK IN THE SKULL'S FAMILY'S HOUSE"

When I saw this lady and when the Skull who brought her to that hole or whom I followed from the market to that hole went to the back-yard, then I changed myself to a man as before, then I talked to the lady but she could not answer me at all, she only showed that she was in a serious condition. The Skull who was guarding her with a whistle fell asleep at that time.

To my surprise, when I helped the lady to stand up from the frog on which she sat, the cowrie that was tied on her neck made a curious noise at once, and when the Skull who was watching her heard the noise, he woke up and blew the whistle to the rest, then the whole of them rushed to the place and surrounded the lady and me, but at the same time that they saw me there, one of them ran to a pit which was not so far from that spot, the pit was filled with cowries. He picked one cowrie out of the pit, after that he was running towards me, and the whole crowd wanted to tie the cowrie on my neck too. But before they could do that, I had changed myself into air, they could not trace me out again, but I was looking at them. I believed that the cowries in that pit were their power and to reduce the power of any human being whenever tied on his or her neck and also to make a person dumb.

Over one hour after I had dissolved into air, these Skulls went back to the back-yard, but there remained the Skull who was watching her.

After they had returned to the back-yard, I changed to a man as usual, then I took the lady from the frog, but at the same time that I touched her, the cowrie which was tied on her neck began to shout; even if a person was four miles away he would not have to listen before hearing, but immediately the Skull who was watching her heard the noise and saw me when I took her from that frog, he blew the whistle to the rest of them who were in the back-yard.

Immediately the whole Skull family heard the whistle when blew to them, they were rushing out to the place and before they could reach there, I had left their hole for the forest, but before I could travel about one hundred yards in the forest, they had rushed out from their hole to inside the forest and I was still running away with the lady. As these Skulls were chasing me about in the forest, they were rolling on the ground like large stones and also humming with terrible noise, but when I saw that they had nearly caught me or if I continued to run away like that, no doubt, they would catch me sooner, then I changed the lady to a kitten and put her inside my pocket and changed myself to a very small bird which I could describe as a "sparrow" in English language.

After that I flew away, but as I was flying in the sky, the cowrie which was tied on that lady's neck was still making a noise and I tried all my best to stop the noise, but all were in vain. When I reached home with the lady, I changed her to a lady as she was before and also myself changed to man as well. When her father saw that I brought his daughter back home, he was exceedingly glad and said thus:—"You are the 'Father of gods' as you had told me before."

But as the lady was now at home, the cowrie on her neck did not stop making a terrible noise once, and she could not talk to anybody; she showed only that she was very glad she was at home. Now I had brought the lady but she could not talk, eat or loose away the cowrie on

28

her neck, because the terrible noise of the cowrie did not allow anybody to rest or sleep at all.

"THERE REMAIN GREATER TASKS AHEAD"

Now I began to cut the rope of the cowrie from her neck and to make her talk and eat, but all my efforts were in vain. At last I tried my best to cut off the rope of the cowrie; it only stopped the noise, but I was unable to loose it away from her neck.

When her father saw all my trouble, he thanked me greatly and repeated again that as I called myself "Father of gods who could do anything in this world" I ought to do the rest of the work. But when he said so, I was very ashamed and thought within myself that if I return to the Skulls' hole or house, they might kill me and the forest was very dangerous travel always, again I could not go directly to the Skulls in their hole and ask them how to loose away the cowrie which was tied on the lady's neck and to make her talk and eat.

"BACK TO THE SKULL'S FAMILY'S HOUSE"

On the third day after I had brought the lady to her father's house, I returned to the endless forest for further investigation. When there remained about one mile to reach the hole of these Skulls, there I saw the very Skull who the lady had followed from the market as a complete gentleman to the hole of Skull's family's house, and at the same time that I saw him like that, I changed into a lizard and climbed a tree which was near him.

He stood before two plants, then he cut a single opposite leaf from the opposite plant; he held the leaf with his right hand and he was saying thus:—"As this lady was taken from me, if this opposite leaf is not given her to eat, she will not talk for ever," after that he threw the leaf down on the ground. Then he cut another single compound leaf from the compound plant which was in the same place with the opposite plant, he held the compound leaf with his left hand and said that if this single compound is not given to this lady, to eat, the cowrie on her neck could not be loosened away for ever and it would be making a terrible noise for ever."

After he said so, he threw the leaf down at the same spot, then he jumped away. So after he had jumped very far away, (luckily, I was there when he was doing all these things, and I saw the place that he threw both leaves separately,) then I changed myself to a man as before, I went to the place that he threw both leaves, then I picked them up and I went home at once.

But at the same time that I reached home, I cooked both leaves separately and gave her to eat; to my surprise the lady began to talk at once. After that, I gave her the compound leaf to eat for the second time and immediately she ate that too, the cowrie which was tied on her neck by the Skull, loosened away by itself, but it disappeared at the same time. So when the father and mother saw the wonderful work which I had done for them, they brought fifty kegs of palm-wine for me, they gave me the lady as wife and two rooms in that house in which to live with them. So, I saved the lady from the complete gentleman in the market who afterwards reduced to a "Skull" and the lady became my wife since that day. This was how I got a wife.

Now as I took the lady as my wife and after I had spent the period of six months with the parents of my wife, then I remembered my palm-wine tapster who had died in my town long ago, then I asked the father of my wife to fulfil his promise or to tell me where my tapster was, but he told me to wait for some time. Because he knew that if he told me the place by that time, I would leave his town and take his daughter away from him and he did not like to part with his daughter.

I spent three years with him in that town, but during that time, I was tapping palm-wine for myself, of course I could not tap it to the quantity that I required to drink; my wife was also helping me to carry it from the farm to the town. When I completed three and a half years in that town, I noticed that the left hand thumb of my wife was swelling out as if it was a buoy, but it did not pain her. One day, she followed me to the farm in which I was tapping the palm-wine, and to my surprise when the thumb that swelled out touched a palm-tree thorn, the thumb bust out suddenly and there we saw a male child came out of it and at the same time that the child came out from the thumb, he began to talk to us as if he was ten years of age.

Within the hour that he came down from the thumb he grew up to the height of about three feet and some inches and his voice by that time was as plain as if somebody strikes an anvil with a steel hammer. Then the first thing that he did, he asked his mother:—"Do you know my name?" His mother said no, then he turned his face to me and asked me the same question and I said no; so, he said that his name was "ZURRJIR" which means a son who would change himself into another thing very soon. But when he told us his name, I was greatly terrified, because of his terrible name, and all the while that he was talking to us, he was drinking the palm-wine which I had tapped already; before five minutes he had drunk up to three kegs out of four kegs. As I was thinking in my mind how we could leave the child in the farm and run to the town, because everybody had seen that the left hand thumb of my wife had only swelled out, but she did not conceive in the right part of her body as other women do. But immediately that I was thinking so, this child took the last keg of palm-wine which he drank through the left of his head and he was going to the town directly, but nobody showed him the road that led to the town. We stood in one place looking at him as he was going, then after a little time, we followed him, but we did not see him on the road before we reached the town. To our surprise the child entered the right house that we were living in. When he entered the house, he saluted everybody that he met at home as if he had known them before, at the same time, he asked for food and they gave him the food, he ate it; after, he entered the kitchen and ate all the food that he met there as well.

But when a man saw him eating the rest of the food

in the kitchen which had been prepared for night, he told him to leave the kitchen; he did not leave but started to fight the man instead of that; this wonderful child flogged the man so that he could not see well before he left the kitchen and ran away, but the child was still in the kitchen.

When all the people in the house saw what the child had done to that man, then all of them started to fight him. As he was fighting with them he was smashing everything on the ground to pieces, even he smashed all the domestic animals to death, still all the people could not conquer him. After a little we came from the farm to the house, but at the same time that he saw us, he left all the people with whom he was fighting and met us, so when we entered the house, he showed us to everybody in the house saying that these were his father and mother. But as he had eaten all the food which had been prepared against the night, then we began to cook other food, but when it was the time to put the food down from the fire, he put it down for himself and at the same time, he began to eat that again as it was very hot, before we could stop him, he had eaten all the food and we tried all our best to take it from him, but we could not do it at all.

This was a wonderful child, because if a hundred men were to fight with him, he would flog them until they would run away. When he sat on a chair, we could not push him away. He was as strong as iron, if he stood on a place nobody could push him off. Now he became our ruler in the house, because sometimes he would say that we should not eat till night and sometimes he would drive us away from the house at mid-night and sometimes he would tell us to lie down before him for more than two hours.

As this child was stronger than everybody in that town, he went around the town and he began to burn the houses of the heads of that town to ashes, but when the people in the town saw his havocs and bad character, they called me (his father) to discuss how we could exile him away from the town, then I told the people that I knew how I would exile him away from the town. So one night, when it was one o'clock in the mid-night, when I noticed that he slept inside the room I put oil around the house and roof, but as it was thatched with leaves and also it was in the dry season, I lighted the house with fire and closed the rest of the windows and doors which he did not close before he slept. Before he woke up, there was a great fire around the house and roof, smoke did not allow him to help himself, so he burnt together with the house to ashes.

When we saw that the child had burnt into ashes all the town's people were very glad and the town was in peace. When I saw that I had seen the end of the child, then I pressed my wife's father to tell me where my palm-wine tapster was and he told me.

"ON THE WAY TO AN UNKNOWN PLACE"

The same day that the father of my wife told me the place that my tapster was, I told my wife to pack all our belongings and she did so, then we woke up early in the morning and started to travel to an unknown place, but when we had travelled about two miles away to that town which we left, my wife said that she forgot her gold trinket inside the house which I had burnt into ashes, she said that she had forgotten to take it away before the house was burnt into ashes. She said that she would go back and take it, but I told her that it would burn into ashes together with the house. She said that it was a metal and it could not burn into ashes and she said that she was going back to take it, and I begged her not to go back, but she refused totally, so when I saw her going back to take it, then I followed her. When we reached there, she picked a stick and began to scratch the ashes with it, and there I saw that the middle of the ashes rose up suddenly and at the same time there appeared a half-bodied baby, he was talking with a lower voice like a telephone.

At the same time that we saw the ashes rise up and change into half-bodied baby, and he was also talking with a lower voice, then we started to go. Then he was telling my wife to take him along with is, to wait and take him, but as we did not stop and take him with us, he then commanded that our eyes should be blinded and we became blinded at the same moment as he said it; still we did not come back and take him, but we were going on, when he saw that we did not come back and take· him, he commanded again that we should stop breathing, truly speaking we could not breathe. When. we could not breathe in or out, we came back and took him along with us. As we were going on the road, he told my wife to carry him by head, and as he was on my

35

wife's head, he was whistling as if he was forty persons. When we reached a village we stopped and bought food from a food-seller to eat as we were very hungry before reaching there, but when we were about to eat the food, the half-bodied baby did not allow us to eat it, instead of that he took the food and swallowed it as a man swallows a pill, so when the food-seller saw him do so, she ran away and left her food there, but when our half-bodied baby saw that the food-seller had left her food, he crept to the food and swallowed it as well.

So this half-bodied baby did not allow us to eat the food, and we did not taste it at all. When the people of that village saw the half-bodied baby with us, they drove us away from the village. Then we started our journey again and when we had travelled about seven miles away from that village, there we reached another town; we stopped there also, and we bought other food there, but this half-bodied baby did not allow us to eat that again. But by that time we were annoyed and we wanted to eat it by force, but he commanded as before and at the same time we became as he commanded, then we left him to swallow it.

When the people of that town saw him there with us again, they drove us away with juju and they said that we were carrying a spirit about and they said that they did not want a spirit in their town. So if we entered any town or village to eat or sleep, they would drive us away at once and our news had been carried to all towns and villages. Now we could not travel the roads unless from bush to bush, because everybody had heard the information that a man and a woman were carrying

36

a half-bodied baby or spirit about and they were looking for a place to put him and run away.

So by this time we were very hungry and then when we were travelling inside the bush, we tried all our efforts to put him down somewhere and run away, but he did not allow us to do that. After we had failed to put him down, we thought that he would sleep at night, but he did not sleep at night at all, and the worst part of it, he did not let my wife put him down once since she had put him on her head; we were longing to sleep heavily, but he did not allow us to do anything except carry him along. All the time that he was on my wife's head, his belly swelled out like a very large tube, because he had eaten too much food and yet he did not satisfy at any time for he could eat the whole food in this world without satisfaction. As we were travelling about in the bush on that night, my wife was feeling overloading of this baby and if we put him on a scale by that time, he would weigh at least 28 lbs; when I saw that my wife had tired of carrying him and she could not carry him any longer, then I took over to carry him along, but before I could carry him to a distance of about one quarter of a mile. I was unable to move again and I was sweating as if I bath in water for overloading, yet this half-bodied baby did not allow us to put him down and rest.

Ah! how could we escape from this half-bodied baby? But God is so good and as we were carrying him to and fro in the bush on that night, we heard as if they were playing music somewhere in that bush and he told us to carry him to the place that we were hearing the music. Before an hour had passed we reached there.

THREE GOOD CREATURES TOOK OVER OUR TROUBLE—THEY WERE:—DRUM, SONG AND DANCE

When we carried him to the place, there we saw the creatures that we called "Drum, Song and Dance" personally and these three creatures were living creatures as ours. At the same time that we reached there the half-bodied baby came down from my head, then we thanked God. But as he came down from my head he joined the three creatures at once. When "Drum" started to beat himself it was just as if he was beaten by fifty men, when "Song" started to sing, it was just as if a hundred people were singing together and when "Dance" started to dance the half-bodied baby started too, my wife, myself and spirits etc., were dancing with "Dance" and nobody who heard or saw these three fellows would not follow them to wherever they were going. Then the whole of us were following the three fellows and dancing along with them. So we followed the three fellows and were dancing for a good five days without eating or stopping once, before we reached a place which was built in the form of a premises by these creatures with mud.

There were two soldiers stood at the front of the premises, but when we reached there with these three fellows, my wife and myself etc., stopped at the entrance of the premises, only the three fellows and our half-bodied baby entered the premises, after that, we, saw them no more. N.B. We did not want to follow them up to that place, but we could not control ourselves as we were dancing along with them.

So nobody in this world could beat drum as Drum himself could beat, nobody could dance as Dance himself could dance and nobody could sing as Song himself could sing. We left these three wonderful creatures by two o'clock in the mid-night. Then after we had left these creatures and our half-bodied baby, we started a fresh journey, but we travelled for two days before we reached a town and stopped there and rested for two days. But we were penniless before reaching there, then I thought within myself how could we get money for our food etc. After a while I remembered my name which was "Father of gods who could do anything in this world". As there was a large river which crossed the main road to that town, then I told my wife to follow me to the river; when reaching there, I cut a tree and carved it into a paddle, then I gave it to my wife and I told her to enter the river with me; when we entered the river, I commanded one juju which was given me by a kind spirit who was a friend of mine and at once the juju changed me to a big canoe. Then my wife went inside the canoe with the paddle and paddling it, she used the canoe as "ferry" to carry passengers across the river, the fare for adults was 3d (three pence) and half fare for children. In the evening time, then I changed to a man as before and when we checked the money that my wife had collected for that day, it was £7: 5: 3d. After that we went back to the town, we bought all our needs.

Next morning we went there by 4 o'clock as well

before the people of that town woke up, so that they might not know the secret and when we reached there, I did as I did yesterday and my wife continued her work as usual, on that day we came back to home by 7 o'clock in the evening. So we stayed in that town for one month and doing the same work throughout that month, when we checked the money that we collected for that month, it was £56: 11: 9d.

Then we left that town with gladness, we started our journey again, but after we had travelled about eighty miles away to that town, then we began to meet gangs of the "highway-men" on the road, and they were troubling us too much. But when I thought over that the danger of the road might result to the loss of our money or both money and our lives, then we entered into bush, but to travel in this bush was very dangerous too, because of the wild animals, and the boa constrictors were uncountable as sand.

"TO TRAVEL BY AIR"

Then I told my wife to jump on my back with our loads, at the same time, I commanded my juju which was given me by "Water Spirit woman" in the "Bush of the Ghosts" (the full story of the "Spirit woman" appeared in the story book of the Wild Hunter in the Bush of the Ghosts). So I became a big bird like an aeroplane and flew away with my wife, I flew for 5 hours before I came down, after I had left the dangerous area, although it was 4 o'clock before I came down, then we began to trek the remaining journey by land or foot. By 8 o'clock p.m. of that day, then we reached the town in which the father of my wife told me that my palm-wine tapster was.

When reaching there, I asked from that town's people about my tapster who had died long ago in my town. But they told me that my tapster had left there over two years. Then I begged them if they could to tell me the town that he was at at present, and I was told that he was now at "Deads' town" and they told me that he was living with deads at the "Deads' town", they told me that the town was very far away and only deads were living there.

Now we could not return where we were coming from (my wife's father's town) we must go to the Deads' town. Then we left that town after the 3rd day that we arrived there; from that town to the Deads' town there was no road or path which to travel, because nobody was going there from that town at all.

"NO ROAD"—"OUGHT TO TRAVEL FROM BUSH TO BUSH TO THE DEADS' TOWN"

The very day that we left that town, we travelled up to forty miles inside the bush, and when it was 6.30 p.m. in the evening, we reached a very thick bush; this bush was very thick so that a snake could not pass through it without hurt.

So we stopped there, because we could not see well again, it was dark. We slept in that bush, but when it

was about two o'clock in the night, there we saw a
creature, either he was a spirit or other harmful creature,
we could not say, he was coming towards us, he was white
as if painted with white paint, he was white from foot
to the topmost of his body, but he had no head or feet
and hands like human-beings and he got one large eye
on his topmost. He was long about $\frac{1}{4}$ of a mile and his
diameter was about six feet, he resembled a white pillar.
At the same time that I saw him coming towards us,
I thought what I could do to stop him, then I remembered
a charm which was given me by my father before he died.

The use of the charm was this:—If I meet a spirit or
other harmful creature at night and if I used it, it would
turn me into a great fire and smoke, so that the harmful
creatures would be unable to reach the fire. Then I used
the charm and it burnt the white creature, but before
he could burn into ashes there we saw about ninety of
the same kind as this long white creature, all of them
were coming to us (fire) and when they reached the fire
(us) the whole of them surrounded it and bent or curved
towards the fire; after that the whole of them were
crying:—"cold! cold! cold" etc., but as they surrounded
the fire, they did not want to leave there, although they
could not do anything to that fire (us). They were only
warming themselves from the fire and they were
exceedingly satisfied with the fire and to stay with it
as long as it could remain there for them. Of course I
thought that as we had turned into the fire, we would be
safe, but not at all. When I thought over that how we
would leave these white creatures, I remembered that
if we began to move, perhaps these white creatures

would go away, because since 1 o'clock a.m., of that night till 10 o'clock a.m. they were still warming themselves from the fire and did not attempt to go where they came from or to go and eat. Of course I could not say definitely whether they were eating creatures or not.

But do not think that as we had turned into the fire we should not feel hungry, for we were feeling hungry too much though we were fire, and if we turned to persons at once, these white creatures would get a chance to kill us or harm us.

Then we began to move, but as we were moving on, these white creatures were also moving with the fire until we left the thick bush, but when we had left there and when we reached a big field, then they went back to their thick bush. But although we did not know it these long white creatures were bound not to trespass on another's bush, and they did not enter into that field at all although they were satisfied with the fire, and the creatures of that field must not enter into their bush either. That was how we got away from the long white creatures.

As we had freed from the white creatures then we started our journey in that field. This field had no trees or palm-trees, only long wild grasses grew there, all resembled corn-plants, the edges of its leaves were as sharp as razor blades and hairy. Then we travelled in that field till 5 o'clock in the evening, after that, we began to look for a suitable place to sleep till morning.

But as we were looking for such place, there we saw a TERMITES' HOUSE which resembled an umbrella and it was 3 feet high and cream in colour. Then we put our loads under it; after that we rested there for a few minutes, then we thought of making fire there with which to cook our food as we were hungry. But as dried sticks were not near that place then we stood up and went further to gather the sticks for the fire, but as we went further there we met an image which knelt down. It was a female in form and it was also cream in colour. After we had collected the sticks, we came back to the termites' house, then we made the fire, cooked our food and ate it; when it was about 8 o'clock in the night, we slept at the foot of the termites' house, but we could not fall asleep, because of fear, and when it was about 11 o'clock of that night we began to hear as if we were in the middle of a market, then we listened to it very well and before we rose up our heads, we were in the centre of a market. Not knowing that it was the owner of the market, that we put our loads on, making fire and also slept under him, but we thought that it was only a termites' house, but no.

Then we started to pack our loads at once to leave the place, perhaps we might be safe, but as we were packing our loads, that field's creatures had surrounded us and caught us like a policeman, so we followed them, and also the termites' house (the owner of the market) under who we slept followed us too, as he was following us, he was jumping, because he had no foot, but a very small head like a one-month-old baby's head, and when we reached the place where the female image knelt down, she stood up and followed us too.

But after we had travelled about twenty minutes, we

44

reacned their king's palace, although he was not in when we reached there at that moment.

The palace was almost covered with refuse, it resembled an old ruined house, it was very rough. When these field creatures saw that the king was not at home, they waited for half an hour before he came, but when we (my wife and I) saw him, he himself was refuse, because he was almost covered with both dried and undried leaves and we could not see his feet and face etc. He entered the palace and at once came and sat down on the refuse. After that his people presented us to him and lodged complaint that we trespassed their town. When they had told him that, he asked them what were these two dulls, but his people said that they could not describe them at all, because they had not seen these kind of creatures before. As my wife and I did not talk a single word by that time, they thought that we were unable to talk, then their king gave one of them a sharp stick to stab us, perhaps we might talk or feel pain; he did as their king told him to do. So as he mercilessly stabbed us with that stick, we felt pain and talked out, but at the same time that the whole of them heard our voice, they laughed at us if bombs explode, and we knew "Laugh" personally on that night, because as every one of them stopped laughing at, "Laugh" did not stop for two hours. As "Laugh" was laughing at us on that night, my wife and myself forgot our pains and laughed with him, because he was laughing with curious voices that we never heard before in our life. We did not know the time that we fell into his laugh, but we were only laughing at "Laugh's" laugh and nobody who heard him

when laughing would not laugh, so if somebody continue to laugh with "Laugh" himself, he or she would
die or faint at once for long laughing, because laugh was
his profession and he was feeding on it. Then they began
to beg "Laugh" to stop, but he could not. Not knowing
that these field creatures had never seen human-beings
before, after a while, their king told them to take us to
their "gods of war". But when I heard that from him,
I was very glad, because I myself was "Father of gods".
These field creatures pushed us to their "gods of war"
as their king said, but they did not go near the "god"
because nobody would and return alive. After they had
pushed us to him and gone back to the market and as the
"god" could talk and I myself was "Father of gods"
also and I had known the secrets of all "gods", so I talked
to this god with a kind of voice, then he did not harm us,
instead he led us out of that field. As their king was
talking, a hot steam was rushing out of his nose and
mouth as a big boiler and he was breathing at five minutes interval. That was how we left the field creatures
and their field.

THE "WRAITH-ISLAND"

Then we started our journey in another bush, of course,
it was full of Islands and swamps and the creatures of
the Islands were very kind, because as soon as we reached
there, they received us with kindness and gave us a
lovely house in their town to live in. The name of the
Island was called "Wraith-Island", it was very high

and it was entirely surrounded by water; all the people of the Island were very kind and they loved themselves, their work was only to plant their food, after that, they had no other work more than to play music and dance. They were the most beautiful creatures in the world of the curious creatures and also the most wonderful dancers and musicians, they were playing music and dancing throughout the day and night. But as the weather of the Island was suitable for us and when we saw that we should not leave there at once, we were dancing with them and doing as they were doing there. Whenever these Island creatures dress, you would be thinking they were human-beings and their children were performing always the stage plays. As we were living with them I became a farmer and planted many kinds of crops. But one day, as the crops had ripened enough there, I saw a terrible animal coming to the farm and eating the crops, but one morning I met him there, so I started to drive him away from the farm, of course I could not approach him as he was as big as an elephant. His fingernails were long to about two feet, his head was bigger than his body ten times. He had a large mouth which was full of long teeth, these teeth were about one foot long and as thick as a cow's horns, his body was almost covered with black long hair like a horse's tail hair. He was very dirty. There were five horns on his head and curved and levelled to the head, his four feet were as big as a log of wood. But as I could not go near him, I stoned him at a long distance, but before the stone could reach him, he had reached where I stood and got ready to fight me.

Then I thought over that how could I escape from

this fearful animal. Not knowing that he was the owner of the land on which I planted the crops, by that critical time, he was angry that I did not sacrifice to him before I planted crops there, but when I understood what he wanted from me, then I cut some of the crops and gave him, so when he saw what I gave him, then he made a sign that I should mount his back and I mounted his back, and by that time I did not hear him any more, then he took me to his house which was not so far from the farm. When we reached there, he bent down and I dismounted from his back, after that he entered his house and brought out four grains of corn, 4 grains of rice and 4 seeds of okra and gave them to me, then I went back to the farm and planted them all at the same time. But to my surprise, these grains and the seeds germinated at once, before 5 minutes they became full grown crops and before 10 minutes again, they had produced fruits and ripened at the same moment too, so I plucked them and went back to the town (the Wraith-Island).

But after the crops had produced the last fruits and when dried, I cut them and kept their seeds as a reference as we were travelling about in the bush.

"NOT TOO SMALL TO BE CHOSEN"

There were many wonderful creatures in the olden days. One day, the king of the "Wraith-Island" town chose all the people, spirits and terrible creatures of the Island to help him to clear his corn field which was about 2 miles square. Then one fine morning, we gathered together and went to the corn field, and cleared it away, after that, we returned to the king and told him that we had cleared his corn field, he thanked us, and gave us food and drinks.

But as a matter of fact none of the creatures is too small to choose for a help. We did not know that immediately we left the field, a tiny creature who was not chosen with us by the king went to the field and commanded all the weeds that we had cleared to grow up as if they were not cleared.

He was saying thus:—"THE KING OF THE 'WRAITH-ISLAND' BEGGED ALL THE CREATURES OF THE 'WRAITH-ISLAND' AND LEFT HIM OUT, SO THAT, ALL THE CLEARED-WEEDS RISE UP; AND LET US GO AND DANCE TO A BAND AT THE 'WRAITH-ISLAND'; IF BAND COULD NOT SOUND, WE SHOULD DANCE WITH MELODIOUS MUSIC."

But at the same time that the tiny creature commanded the weeds, all rose up as if the field was not cleared for two years. Then early in the morning of the second day that we had cleared it, the king went to the field to visit his corn, but to his surprise, he met the field uncleared, then he returned to the town and called the whole of us and asked that why did we not clear his field? We replied that we had cleared it yesterday, but the king said no, we did not clear it. Then the whole of us went to the field to witness it, but we saw the field as if it was not cleared as the king said. After that we gathered together and went to clear it as before, then we returned to the king again and told him that we had cleared it. But when he went there, he found it uncleared as before and came back to the town and told us again that we did not clear his field, then the whole of us ran to the field and found it uncleared. So we gathered together for the third time and went to clear it, after we had cleared it, we told one of us to hide himself inside a bush which was very close to the field, but before 30 minutes that he was watching the field, he saw a very tiny creature who was just a baby of one day of age and he commanded the weeds to rise up as he was commanding before. Then that one of us who hid himself inside the bush and was watching him tried all his efforts and caught him, then he brought him to the king; when the king saw the tiny creature, he called the whole of us to his palace.

After that, the king asked him who was commanding the cleared-weeds of his field to rise up after the field had been cleared: The tiny creature replied that he was commanding all the weeds to rise up, because the king chose all the creatures of the "Wraith-Island" town but left him out, although he was the smallest among all, but he had the power to command weeds etc. which had been cleared to grow up as if it was not cleared at all. But the king said that he had just forgotten to choose him with the rest and not because of his small appearance.

Then the king made excuses to him, after that he went away. This was a very wonderful tiny creature.

After we (my wife and I) had completed a period of 18 months in this "Wraith-Island", then I told them that we wished to continue our journey, because we were not reaching our destination at all. But as the creatures of this Island were very kind, they gave my wife many expensive articles as gifts then we packed all our loads and when it was early in the morning, the whole people of the "Wraith-Island" led us with a big canoe and they were singing the song of "good-bye" as they were·paddling along on the river. When they accompanied us to their boundary, they stopped, but when we went down from their canoe, then they returned to their town with a lovely song and music and bade us good-bye. If it was in their power, they would have led us to our destination, but they were forbidden to touch another creature's land or bush.

While we had enjoyed everything in that "Wraith-Island", to our satisfaction, there were still many great tasks ahead. Then we started our journey in another bush, but remember that there was no road on which to travel in those bushes at all.

As we entered the bush, when we had travelled for about 2 miles inside the bush, then we began to notice that there were many trees without withered leaves, dried sticks and refuse on the ground of this bush as was usual in other bushes; as we were very hungry before reaching there, we put down our loads at the foot of a tree. Then we looked around the tree for pieces of dried wood with which to make a fire, but nothing was found there; to our surprise, there was a sweet smelling in every part of the bush, the smelling was just as if they were baking cakes, bread and roasting of fowls or meat; God was so good, we began to snuff the sweet smelling and we were very satisfied with it and we did not feel hungry again. That bush was very "greedy", so that within an hour from when we sat at the foot of the tree, the ground on which we sat began to warm and we could not sit on it any longer, then we took our loads and went further.

As we were going on in this bush, we saw a pond and we branched there, then we started to drink the water from it, but as the water dried away at our presence and also as we were thirsty all the time, and there we saw that there was not a single living creature. But when we saw that the ground of this bush was very hot for us to stand, sit or to sleep on till morning and again the bush did not like anybody to remain there any longer than necessary, then we left there and went further, but as we were going on, we saw again many palm-trees without leaves, but only small birds represented the leaves, all these palm-trees were in a row. The first one that we reached was very tall and as we appeared to him, he laughed, then the second to him asked what was making him laugh; he replied that he saw two living creatures in their bush today, but as soon as we got to the second he also laughed at us too so loudly that as if a person was five miles away would hear, then the whole of them were laughing at us together and the whole of that bush was just as if it was full of a big market's noises as they were in the same row. But when I rose up my head and looked at the top of them I noticed that they had heads, and the heads were artificial heads, but they were talking as human-beings, although they were talking with curious language, and the whole of them were smoking very big and long smoking pipes as they were looking at us, of course, we could not say where they got the pipes. We were so very curious to them as they had never seen human-beings before.

As we were thinking to sleep there, we were unable to sleep or stay for their noise and laughing. After we had left the "Greedy-Bush", then we entered into a forest at about 1.30 in the mid-night, then we slept under a tree till morning and nothing happened to us throughout that night, but we had not eaten anything since the day that we had left the "Wraith-Island", the most beautiful Island in the world of the curious creatures. When it was dawn we woke up under the tree and made a fire with which we cooked our food and ate it there, but before we finished with the food, we saw that animals of that forest were running to and fro, we saw a lot of birds were chasing the animals up and down, these birds were eating the flesh of the animals; the birds were about 2 feet long and their beaks were also one foot and very sharp as a sword.

When these birds started to eat the flesh of those animals, within a second there we saw about 50 holes on the bodies of those animals and within a second the animals fell down and died, but when they began to eat the dead bodies it did not last them more than 2 minutes before they finished them (bodies) and as soon as they had eaten that, they would start to chase others about. But when these birds saw us where we sat down they were looking at us fiercely and also with astonishment, but when I thought that these might set us as they were eating the animals, then I gathered dried leaves and set fire to them, after that I put on it juju-power which was given me by my friend who was the two-headed creature in the "Bush of the Ghosts, 2nd Country of the Ghosts". The smelling powder drove all these birds away for a few minutes. So we could travel in that forest by day as far as we could. But when it was night, we sat down under a tree and laid down our loads; we were sitting down and sleeping under trees whenever it was night as a shelter. As we sat down under this tree and were thinking about that night's danger, there we saw a "Spirit of Prey", he was big as hippopotamus, but he was walking upright as a human-being; his both legs had two feet and tripled his body, his head was just like a lion's head and every part of his body was covered with hard scales, each of these scales was the same in size as a shovel or hoe, and all curved towards his body. If this "Spirit of Prey" wanted to catch his prey, he would simply be looking at it and stand in one place, he was not chasing his prey about, and when he focused the prey well, then he would close his large eyes, but before he would open his eyes, his prey would be already dead and drag itself to him at the place that he stood. When this "Spirit of Prey" came nearer to the place where we slept on that night, he stood at about 80 yards away from us, and looked at us with his eyes which brought out a flood-light like mercury in colour.

As that light was shining on us, we at once began to feel heat as if we had bathed with water, even my wife fainted of this heat. But I was praying to God by that time not to let this "Spirit of Prey" close his eyes, because if he closed them, no more, we had perished there. But God is so good he did not remember to close his eyes by that time, and I myself was feeling the heat of his eyes too much and also I nearly fainted with suffocation. Then I saw a buffalo which was passing that way at that time, then this "Spirit of Prey" closed his eyes as usual and the buffalo died and dragged itself to him, after that he began to eat it. So by that time I got a chance to escape from him, but when I remembered that my wife had fainted then I looked around the place where we sat and saw a tree with many branches, then I climbed it with my wife and left our loads at the foot of that tree. To my surprise, he had eaten off the dead body of the buffalo within four minutes and at once he pointed the flood-light of his eyes towards the place where we sat before we climbed the tree; he found nothing there but our loads. So when he directed the flood-light of his eyes to the loads, the loads dragged themselves to him but when he loosened the loads, he found nothing edible there. After that, he waited for us till the day was nearly breaking and when he saw that he could not get us any more, then he went away.

As I was treating my wife throughout that night, she was very well before early in the morning. Then we got down from the tree and packed our loads and we started our journey at once. Before 5 p.m. we had left that bush behind. That was how we were saved from the "Spirit of Prey" etc.

We started our journey in another bush with new creatures, this bush was smaller than that one which we had passed behind and it was also a various bush, because there we met many houses which had been ruined for hundreds of years and all the properties of those who had left there remained as if they were using them every day; there we saw an image which sat down on a flat stone, it had two long breasts with deep eyes, it was very ugly and terrible to see. After that we went further in this ruined town and saw another image with a full basket of colas on its front, then I took out one of the colas, but to our surprise, at the same time that I took it, we heard a voice of somebody suddenly, which said:— DON'T TAKE IT! LEAVE IT THERE! but I did not listen to the voice that we heard. Immediately I had taken the cola, we kept going, and again to our surprise, there we saw a man who was walking towards his back or backwards, his both eyes were on his knees, his both arms were at his both thighs, these both arms were longer than his feet and both could reach the topmost of any tree; and he held a long whip too. He was chasing us as we were going on hastily with that whip, so by that time, we started to run for our life, but he was chasing us to and fro in that bush for two hours; he wanted to flog us with that whip. But as we were running away from this creature, we entered into a wide road unexpectedly, as we entered the road, he got back from us at once, although we could not say, whether he was bound to trek on that road.

When we reached this road, we waited for thirty minutes; perhaps we might see somebody pass, because we did not know to which side of the two to travel, again the road might not be there at all. But though we waited for 30 minutes there, nobody passed, even a fly did not fly on it.

As the road was very clean, we noticed that a foot mark could not be traced, then we believed that it was the road which led to the—"UNRETURNABLE-HEAVEN'S TOWN" the town in which human-beings or other creatures were bound to enter; if anybody entered it, no doubt he or she would not return again, because the inhabitants of the town were very bad, cruel and merciless.

ON OUR WAY TO THE UNRETURNABLE-HEAVEN'S TOWN

Now we followed this road from the north side and we were very glad to be travelling on it, but still no trace of foot mark or of anybody met on the way. As we travelled along it from two o'clock till seven o'clock in the evening without reaching a town or the end, then we stopped at the roadside and made a fire there; we cooked our food and ate it there and slept there as well, but nothing happened to us throughout the night. When it was dawn we woke up and cooked our food and ate it.

After that we started our journey, but although we had travelled from that morning till 4 o'clock in the evening, yet we did not see or meet anybody on this road, then we were quite sure that it was "Unreturnable-Heaven's town" road, so we did not go further; we stopped and slept there till the morning. Very early in the morning, we woke and prepared our food and ate it, after that, we thought to go on a little bit before we should leave the road.

But as we were going on and when it was time that we wanted to branch to our left, to continue the journey inside another bush as usual, we were unable to branch or to stop, or to go back, we were only moving on the road towards the town. We tried all our best to stop ourselves but all were in vain.

How could we stop now was the question that we asked ourselves, because we were approaching the town. Then I remembered one of my juju which had escaped me and I performed it to stop us, but instead of that, we started to move faster than before. When there remained one quarter of a mile to reach the town, we came to a large gate which crossed the road, it was closed then. When we reached the gate, then we could stop, but we could not move to front or back, We stood before this gate for about 3 hours before it opened itself, then we moved to the town unexpectedly and we did not know who was pushing us. When we entered this town we saw creatures that we had never seen in our life and I could not describe the whole of them here, but however, I should tell some of their stories which went thus:— This town was very big and full of unknown creatures, both adults and children were very cruel to human-beings, and yet they were looking for ways of making their cruelties even worse; as soon as we entered their town, six of them held us firmly and the rest were beating us and also their children were stoning us repeatedly.

These unknown creatures were doing everything incorrectly, because there we saw that if one of them wanted to climb a tree, he would climb the ladder first before leaning it against that tree; and there was a flat land near their town but they built their houses on the side of a steep hill, so all the houses bent downwards as if they were going to fall, and their children were always rolling down from these houses, but their parents did not care about that; the whole of them did not wash their bodies at all, but washed their domestic animals; they wrapped themselves with a kind of leaves as their clothes, but had costly clothes for their domestic animals, and cut their domestic animals' finger nails, but kept their own uncut for one hundred years; even there we saw many of them sleeping on the roofs of their houses and they said that they could not use the houses that they built with their hands except to sleep on them.

Their town was surrounded with a thick and tall wall. If any earthly person mistakenly entered their town, they would catch him or her and begin to cut the flesh of his or her body into pieces while still alive, sometimes they would stab a person's eyes with a pointed knife and leave it there until that person would die of much pain. As six of them held us firmly, they were taking us to their king, but as we were taken along, the rest and their children were beating and stoning us. But as we wanted to enter the palace of their king, there we met uncountable of them at the gate of their king's palace and waiting for to beat. When we entered the palace, they handed us to the king's attendants. After the attendants took us to the king, but as we were inside the palace, thousands of them were waiting for us at the gate of the palace, some of them held clubs, knives, cutlasses and other fighting weapons and all their children held stones.

The questions that their king asked us went thus:— From where were you coming? I replied that we were coming from the earth. He asked again how did we manage to reach their town? I replied that it was their road brought us to the town and we did not want to come there at all. After that he asked us where were we going to? Then I replied that we were going to my palm-wine tapster's town who had died in my town sometime ago. As I had said already that these unknown creatures were very cruel to anybody that mistakenly entered their town, as I answered all the questions, he repeated the name of their town for us again—"Unreturnable-Heaven's town." He said:—a town in which are only enemies of God living, only cruel, greedy and merciless creatures. After he said so, he commanded his attendants to clear all the hair from our heads, but when the attendants and the people at the gate heard that from their king, they jumped up with gladness and shouted. God is so good, that the attendants did not take us to the outside of the palace before they started to shave our heads as the king ordered them, otherwise we would be torn into pieces by the people waiting for us at the gate of the palace.

Then the king gave them flat stones to use as razor blades, and as the attendants were clearing the hair with the flat stones, the flat stones were unable to clear the hair as razor blades would and only hurt every part of our heads After they had tried all their efforts and failed, then the king gave them pieces of broken bottle to use, when they got that, it cleared some of the hair by force, and blood did not allow them to see the rest of our hair again. But before they started to shave off the hair, they had tied us with strong ropes to one of the pillars of that palace. After they had cleared some of the hair, they left us there unloosened and went to grind pepper, after a while, they brought the pepper and rubbed our heads with it, then they lighted a thick rag with fire and tied it on the centre of our heads so that it nearly touched our heads. By that time, we did not know whether we were still alive or dead, although we could not defend our heads, because both our hands and bodies were tied to that pillar. When it was about half an hour since they had hung the fire near our heads, they took it away and started to scrape our heads again with a big snail's shell, so by that time, every part of the heads was bleeding; but before that time all the people that were waiting for us at the gate had returned to their houses, tired of long waiting.

After that, they took us to a wide field which was in the full heat of the sun, there were no trees or shadow near there and it was cleared as a football field; it was near the town. Then they dug two pits or holes side by side, in size of which would reach the jaw of a person, in the centre of the field. After that they put me into one and my wife into the second and replaced the earth that they had dug out and pressed it hard in such a way that we could hardly breathe. Then they put food near our mouths, but we were unable to touch or eat it; they knew that we were very hungry by that time. And after that, the whole of them cut whips and began to flog our heads, but we had no hands to defend our heads. At last they brought an eagle before us to take out our eyes with its beak, but the eagle was simply looking at our eyes, it did no harm to us. Then these people went back to their houses and left the eagle there with us. But as I had tamed such a bird in my town before I left there, so this one did not harm us at all and we remained in these

holes from three o'clock p.m. till morning and at about
9 o'clock of that morning the sun came and shone severely
on us; when it was 10 o'clock, these people came again
and made a big fire around us and flogged us for some
minutes, then they went away. But when the fire was
about to quench, their children came with whips and
stones then they began to whip and stone our heads;
when they left that, they began to climb on our heads
and jump from one to the second; after that they started
to spit, make urine and pass excreta on our heads; but
when that eagle saw that they wanted to nail our heads,
then it drove all of them away from the field with its
beak. But before that people (adults) left, they scheduled
the time that they would come and pay us the last visit
for 5 o'clock in the evening of the second day that we
were in those holes. God is so good, when it was 3 o'clock
p.m., a heavy rain came and it rained till a late hour in
the night and it disappointed them from coming to pay
the last visit.

As it rained heavily, when it was one o'clock in the
night, the holes became soft, so when that eagle saw us
trying to get out of the holes, it came nearer and began
to scratch the hole in which I was, but as the holes were
very deep, it could not scratch it out as quickly as it
wanted to. But when I shook my body to left and right,
then I got out and ran to my wife and pulled her out of
her own too. Then we hastily left that field and went
to the main gate of the town, but unluckily, we found
it closed and the town was entirely surrounded by a thick
and tall wall, so we hid ourselves under a bush which
had not been cleared for long time and was near the

wall. When the day broke the people came to the field and found nothing there; after that they began to search for us and when they reached the bush in which we hid ourselves, they were smashing it together with us, so when they could not trace us out they thought that we had left their town.

As the sun of that town was very hot, every place dried early; when it was about two o'clock in the midnight, and when the whole of them slept, then we went into the town cautiously and took some fire from their fire which was not yet quenched. All their houses were thatched with grasses and also it was in the dry season, as again the houses touched each other, then we lighted some of the houses with the fire; it caught fire at once and before they could wake up, all the houses had burnt into ashes and about ninety per cent of them also burnt with the houses and none of their children were saved. Then the rest of them that were saved, stole away that night.

When it was dawn, then we went to the town and found nobody there, so we took one of their sheep and killed it, then roasted it, after that, we ate as much of it as we could and packed the rest and took one of their axes and left the town empty, so when we reached the thick wall, I cut a part of it like a window and passed out through that place.

That was how we were saved from the Unknown creatures of the "Unreturnable-Heaven's town". After we had left that town very far away and believed that we were freed from the unknown creatures, then we stopped and built a small temporary house inside the bush in which we were travelling along, it was built in form of an upstairs and thatched with grasses, then I surrounded it with sticks as fence, so that it might keep us from the animals etc. Then I began to treat my wife there. In the daytime, I would go around the bush, I should kill bush animals, after that I should pick edible fruits and we were feeding on them as food. When we completed the period of three months there for treatment, my wife was very well, but as I was roaming about in that bush in search of animals, there I discovered an old cutlass which had had its wooden handle eaten off by insects, then I took it and coiled it round with the string of a palm-tree, then I sharpened it on a hard ground, because there was no stone, and cut a strong and slender stick and then bent it in form of a bow and sharpened many small sticks as arrows, so I was defending ourselves with it. But after we had completed the period of five months and some days in that house, we thought that to go back to the town of my wife's father was dangerous, because of various punishments, and we could not trace out the right way on which we travelled from that place again. To go back was harder and to go further was the hardest, so at last we made up our mind and started to go forward. In case of emergency, I took the bow and arrows with the cutlass with us, but we had no other load more than that, because our loads had been taken from us in the town of "Unreturnable-Heaven's", and of course we had burnt our loads together with their houses. Then we started our journey very early in the morning, but it was a very dark day which seemed as if rain was coming heavily. After we had travelled about

seven miles from that house which we left, then we
stopped and ate some of the roasted meat which we took
along with us. After that we started to travel again, but
we did not travel more than a mile in that bush before
we reached a large river which crossed our way to pass;
when we reached there, we could not enter it, because
it was very deep as we were looking at it and noticing
that there was no canoe or other thing with which to
cross it. When we had stopped there for a few minutes,
we travelled to our right along the bank of this river as
perhaps we might reach the end of it, but we travelled
more than four miles without seeing the end at all. Then
we turned back and travelled to our left again. When we
had travelled about six miles away without seeing the
end, then we stopped to think what we could do to cross
the river. But at that moment we thought to go further
along the bank perhaps we could reach the end or a
safe place to rest or sleep at night. As we were going
further, we did not travel more than one third of a mile
on this river-bank, before we saw a big tree which was
about one thousand and fifty feet in length and about
two hundred feet in diameter. This tree was almost white
as if it was painted every day with white paint with all
its leaves and also branches. As we were about forty
yards away from it, there we noticed that somebody
peeped out and was focusing us as if a photographer was
focusing somebody. So, at the same time we saw him
focusing us like that, we started to run to our left, but
he turned to that place too, and we turned to our right
again, and he did so, and still focusing us like that and
we did not see who was focusing us, but only that tree

65

which was turning as we were doing. After we had seen this terrible tree which was focusing us, then we said that we should not wait for this again, then we were running away for our life at once. But immediately we were running away from this tree, we heard a terrible voice suddenly as if many persons talked into a big tank, then we looked at our back and there we saw two large hands which came out from the tree and made a sign of "STOP," but directly we saw him saying so, we did not stop at all, after that he said again—"STOP-THERE AND COME-HERE" but still, we did not go to him as he said. He told us again with another curious and larger voice to stop, but that time we stopped and looked at our back.

But as we looked at our back, we were looking at the large hands with fear, so when the hands gave us sign to come to him, now my wife and myself betraited ourselves, because when the hands told both of us to come to him, my wife pointed me to the hands and I myself pointed her to the hands too; after that, my wife forced me to go first and I pushed her to go first. As we were doing that, the hands told us again that both of us were wanted inside the tree, so when we thought that we had never seen a tree with hands and talking in our life, or since we have been travelling in the bushes, then we started to run away as before, but to our surprise, when the hands saw that we took to our heels again, they stretched out from the tree without end and then picked both of us off the ground as we were running away. After that they were drawing back to the inside of the tree, but when we nearly touched the tree, there we

66

saw that a large door opened and the hands drew us through that door to the inside of the tree.

Now by that time and before we entered inside the white tree, we had 'sold our death' to somebody at the door for the sum of £70: 18: 6d and 'lent our fear' to somebody at the door as well on interest of £3: 10: 0d per month, so we did not care about death and we did not fear again. When we entered inside the white tree, there we found ourselves inside a big house which was in the centre of a big and beautiful town, then the hands directed us to an old woman, and after the hands disappeared. So we met the old woman sat on a chair in a big parlour which was decorated with costly things, then she told us to sit down before her and we did so. Then she asked us did we know her name; we said no; then she said that her name was called "FAITHFUL-MOTHER" and she told us that she was only helping those who were in difficulties and enduring punishments but not killing anybody.

After that, she asked us did we know the name of the big hands who brought us to her; we said no. Then she told us that the big hands' name was called "FAITHFUL-HANDS," she said that the work of Faithful-hands was to watch out for those wo were passing or going about in their bush with difficulties etc. and bring them to her.

"THE WORK OF THE FAITHFUL-MOTHER
IN THE WHITE TREE"

After she had related her story, then she told one of her servants to give us food and drinks and at the same time the servant served us with the food and drinks, but after we had eaten and drank to our satisfaction, then the Faithful-Mother told us to follow her and we did so. She took us to the largest dancing hall which was in the centre of that house, and there we saw that over 300 people were dancing all together. The hall was decorated with about one million pounds (£) and there were many images and our own too were in the centre of the hall. But our own images that we saw there resembled us too much and were also white colour, but we were very surprised to meet our images there, perhaps somebody who was focusing us as a photographer at the first time before the hands drew us inside the white tree had made them, we could not say. So we asked from Faithful-Mother what she was doing with all of the images. She replied that, they were for remembrance and to know those she was helping from their difficulties and punishments. This beautiful hall was full of all kinds of food and drinks, over twenty stages were in that hall with uncountable orchestras, musicians, dancers and tappers. The orchestras were always busy. The children of seven to eight years etc. of age were always dancing, tapping on the stage with melodious songs and they were also singing with warm tones with non-stop dance till morning. There we saw that all the lights in this hall were in technicolours and they were changing colours at five minutes intervals. After that she took us to the dining hall and then to the kitchen in which we met about three hundred and forty cooks who were always busy as bees and all the rooms in this house were in a row. Then she took us to her hospital where we met again many patients on sick beds and she handed us to one of the patentees to treat our heads without hair which the people of the "Unreturnable-Heaven's town" had cleared with broken bottle by force.

We remained in that hospital for a week under treatment before our heads brought out full-grown hair, then we went back to the Faithful-Mother and she gave us a room.

OUR LIFE WITH THE FAITHFUL-MOTHER IN THE WHITE TREE.

Now we were living with the Faithful-Mother and she was taking care of us with her faithfulness, but within a week that we were living with this mother, we had forgotten all our past torments and she told us to go to the hall at any time we liked. So early in the morning, we should go to the hall and begin to eat and drink, because we were not buying anything that we wanted, so that I began to lavish all the drinks as I had been a great palm-wine drinkard in my town before I left. And within one month my wife and I became good dancers. This was rather queer. One night, when we were short of drinks at about two o'clock in the midnight, then the Chief waiter reported to the Faithful-

Mother that we were short of drinks and there was none in the store, then she gave the chief waiter a small bottle which was exactly the size of injection's bottle and it contained only a little quantity of wine. After the chief waiter brought it to the hall we began to drink it, but for three days and nights, the whole of us could not drink the wine which the bottle contained to one-fifth. So after about three months that we were inside this white tree, we became the inhabitants of the house and we were feeding on anything that we liked free of charge. There was a special room in this house to play gamble and I joined the gang, but I was not perfect enough, so that all the money for which I sold our 'death' was taken away from me by the expert gamblers, but I had forgotten that one day, we should leave there and need money to spend. Of course the borrower of our 'fear' was paying us regularly every month. Now we disliked to continue our journey to the town that we were going to before we entered inside the white tree, as a matter of fact we did not like to leave there ever.

But after we had completed the period of one year and two weeks with Faithful-Mother, one night she called my wife and me and told us that it was time for us to leave there and continue our journey as usual. When she said this we begged her not to let us leave there ever, then she replied that she had no right to delay anybody more than a year and some days, she said again that if that had been in her power, she would grant our request. After that, she told us to go and pack all our loads and be ready to leave there tomorrow morning. Then we went back to our room, and began to think that we were going to start our punishments again. We did not go to the hall that night and we did not sleep till the daybreak, so early in the morning we thought within ourselves to tell her to escort us to our destination. Then we went to her and told her we were ready to leave and we wanted her to lead us to our destination because of fearful creatures in the bush. But she told us that she could not do such request, because she must not go beyond their boundary. So she gave me a gun and ammunitions and a cutlass, then she gave my wife many costly clothes etc. as gifts and gave us plenty of roasted meat with drinks and cigarettes. After that she accompanied us, but what made us very surprised was that we saw the tree opened as a large door, and we simply found ourselves inside the bush unexpectedly, and the door closed at once and the tree seemed as an ordinary tree which could not open like that. But at the same time that we found ourselves at the foot of this white tree inside the bush, both of us (my wife and I) said suddenly "We are in the bush again." Because it was just as if a person slept in his or her room, but when he woke up, he found himself or herself inside a big bush.

Then we took our 'fear' back from the borrower and he paid us the last interest on it. Then we found the one who had bought our 'death' and told him to bring it, but he told us that he could not return it again, because he bought it from us and had paid for it already, so we left our 'death' for the buyer, so we took only our 'fear'. So when the Faithful-Mother led us to the river which we could not cross before we saw the white tree

71

and entered it, we stopped and looked at her. After a while, she picked up a small stick like a match stick on the ground and she threw it on that river, but at the same moment, there we found a narrow bridge which crossed the river to the other edge. Then she told us to cross it to the other edge or the second side, but she stood in the same place, at the same time that we reached the end of the other edge, she stretched out her hand and touched the bridge, but it was only that stick we saw in her hand. After that she was singing and waving her hand to us and we were doing the same thing to her as well, then she disappeared at once. That was how we left the Faithful-Mother in the white tree who was faithful to every creature.

So we took our 'fear' back and started our journey as usual, but before an hour passed since we had left the Faithful-Mother, a heavy rain came and we were beaten by the rain for two hours before it stopped, as there was no shelter in this bush for rain or anything. My wife could not travel as quickly as we wished to, so we stopped and ate the roasted meat which the Faithful-Mother gave us, and we rested there for two hours, then we started to travel again. But as we were travelling along in this bush, we met a young lady who was coming towards us, but as we saw her, we bent to another way, but she bent to the place too, then we stopped for her to come and do anything that she wanted to do, because we had sold our 'death' and we could not die again, but we feared her because we did not sell our 'fear'. When this lady approached us, we noticed that she was dressed in a long fancy gown, and there were many gold-beads

72

around her neck and she wore high-heel shoes which resembled aluminium in colour, she was as tall as a stick of about ten feet long, she was of deep red complexion. After she had approached us, she stopped and asked where we were going to. We replied that we were going to "Dead's town," and she asked again from where were we coming. We replied that we were coming from the Faithful-Mother in the white tree. After we had told her that, then she told us to follow her, but when she said so, we feared her and my wife said—"This is not a human-being and she is not a spirit, but what is she?" Then we were following her as she told us. After we had travelled with her to a distance of about 6 miles in this bush, then we entered inside a "Red-Bush" and the bush was in deep red together with all the trees, ground and all the living creatures therein. Immediately we entered this "Red-Bush" my wife and myself turned deep-red as that bush, but at the same time that we entered the "Red-Bush", these words came out from my wife's mouth—"This is only fear for the heart but not dangerous to the heart."

"WE AND THE RED-PEOPLE IN THE RED-TOWN"

After we had travelled about 12 miles away in the "Red-Bush" with the Red-lady, we entered a Red-town and there we saw that both people and their domestic animals were deep-red in colour. So we entered a house which was the largest in that area, but as we were feeling hungry before reaching there, we asked the lady to give us food and water. After a while she brought both for us, but to our surprise, both food and water were as red as red paint, but both tasted as ordinary food and water so we ate the food and drank the water also. After she had brought the food for us, she left us there and went away, but as we sat down there, these Red-people were coming and looking at us with astonishment. After a few minutes the lady came back and told us to follow her and we did so. Then she took us around the town and showed us everything, after that she took us to their king who was also red as blood. The king saluted us well and told us to sit down before him. Then he asked us where were we coming from? We replied that we were coming from the Faithful-Mother who was in charge of the white tree. When he heard so from us, he said that the Faithful-Mother was his sister, then we told him how she helped us from our difficulties etc. After that he asked us what was the name of our town. We told him the name. Then he asked whether we were still alive or dead before coming there. We told him that we were still alive and we were not deads.

After that he told the Red-lady that brought us to him to put us in one of the rooms in his palace, but the room was very far from the other rooms and nobody was living near there. So we entered the room and began to think— What was his aim, the Red-king of the Red-people in the Red-town, was the question we asked ourselves, and we could not sleep till morning, because of this question.

When it was early in the morning, we went to the Red-king and sat down before him and waited for what he would say. But when it was about 8 o'clock, the Red-lady who brought us to the Red-king came and sat down behind us. After a while the Red-king started the story of the Red-town, Red-people, and the Red-Bush thus:— He said—"The whole of us in this Red-town were once human-beings; in the olden days when the eyes of all the human-beings were on our knees, when we were bending down from the sky because of its gravitiness and when we were walking backwards and not forwards as nowadays."

He said also "One day, when I was still among the human-beings I set one trap in a bush which was very far away from any river, even a pond did not be near there, then I set one fish-net inside a river which was very far away from any bush, even a piece of land did not be near there. But when it was next morning, I went first to the river in which I set the fish-net for fish, but to my surprise, the net had caught a red-bird instead of a fish and the red-bird was still alive as it was in a river. Then I took out the net together with the red-bird and put it down on the bank of the river. Next I went to the bush in which I had set the trap for bush animals and again the trap had also caught a big red fish and it was still alive. After that, I took both the net and the trap with red-bird and red fish to my town. But when my parents saw the red fish that the trap caught instead of a bush animal and again that the fish-net had caught a red-bird instead of a fish, and both were still alive, they told me to return them to the place that I brought them from, and I took both of them and returned to put them in the place where I had caught them.

But when I was going along the way, I stopped midway under the shade of a tree and made a fire there, then I put these two red creatures inside the fire. My aim was to burn them into ashes and return to my town from there. But what surprised me most was that, when I was going to put these red creatures in the fire, they were talking like human-beings, saying that I must not put them in the fire, because red creatures were not to go near fire at all, but when I heard that from them, I was greatly terrified. Of course, I did not listen to them, I was only taking both of them from the net and trap to the fire, but as I was taking them out of the net and trap, they were still boasting that I could not put them in that fire at all. Although when I heard that from them, I was greatly annoyed and put them in that fire by force. As these red creatures were inside that fire, they were saying that I should take them out of the fire at once, but I told them that that could not be done at all. After a little time, they burnt into halves, but they were still talking. Then I gathered more dried sticks and put them inside the fire, but when the fire rose up, I was suddenly covered by the smoke which came out from the fire, and I could hardly breathe. Before I could find my way out from the smoke I had turned red, and when I saw that I had become red, then I ran to my town and entered our house, but the smoke was following me as I was running to our house, and entered the house with me. When my parents saw that I had turned into red, they wanted to wash me, perhaps the red would be washed away, but as soon as the smoke entered with me the whole people became red also, then we went before the king who was on the throne to show him what had happened, but the smoke did not allow the king to say anything, before it scattered all over the town and all the people, domestic animals, town, river and bush became red at the same time.

But when everyone of us had failed to wash his or her red away, then on the 7th day after we had turned into the red the whole of us died with our domestic animals, and we left that town and settled down here, but we were still red as before we died and also our domestic animals, rivers, town and bush or anything we met here became red, so that since that time we were called Red-people and our town was called Red-town etc. But some days after we had settled down here, the red fish and the red-bird came and lived inside a big hole which was very near this town. Since both red creatures came here they have been coming out from the hole every year for human sacrifice and we are sacrificing one of us to them yearly to save the rest of us. So we are very glad that both of you came to the Red-town just now because there remain only three days before these two creatures come out for their sacrifice of this year and I should be very glad too if one of you would volunteer his or her life for these two creatures."

After the Red-king had related the story for us and in his conclusion had said that one of us should volunteer his or her life for the two creatures, willingly or not, I asked my wife what could we do now? Because I do not want to leave her or she to leave me here alone and none of these Red-people wanted to volunteer his or her life for these creatures and again the king wanted to hear from us as soon as possible.

But my wife said these words—"This would be a brief loss of woman, but a shorter separation of a man from lover." But I did not understand the meaning of her words, because she was talking with parables or as a foreteller. After a little time I went to the Red-king and told him that I should volunteer my life for the two red creatures. And when the Red-king and Red-people heard that from me, they were exceedingly glad. The reason why I volunteered my life was that when I remembered that we had sold away our 'death' to somebody, I knew these two creatures would be unable to kill me at all. I did not know that these Red-people would perform their native ceremony for me or anybody who volunteers his or her life to the two creatures before the very day that the two creatures would come out from their hole.

Now the Red-people removed all the hair of my head and painted the half part of it with a kind of red paint and the other part with white native paint, after that, the whole of them gathered together and put me on their front with their drummers and singers. They told me to dance as the drummers were beating their drums around the town. My wife was also following us, but she did not show that she would lose me soon at all. But when it was 5 o'clock early in the morning that the two red creatures would come out, I took my gun, ammunitions and cutlass which the Faithful-Mother gave me before we left her, then I loaded the gun with the most powerful ammunitions and put it on my shoulder and sharpened the cutlass and held it firmly with my right hand. When it was 7 o'clock of that morning, the Red-king and all the Red-people took me to the place where the hole was, and put me there for the red creatures, then the whole of them went back to the town. The place was not more than half a mile from the town.

They left me there alone and ran back to the town, because if the two red creatures should see more than one person whom they give them as sacrifice, they would kill them as well. But my wife did not return to the town with them, she hid herself near the place I was but I did not know at all. When it was half an hour that I stood before the hole, I began to hear that something was making a noise as if it was a thousand persons in that hole, every part of that place was shaking, by that time I took only my gun from my shoulder and held it firmly, then I sighted the hole. But when these two red creatures were coming out from the hole, they did not walk side by side but following each other and when the one at the front appeared and was coming towards me, it was red fish in form. As a matter of fact, when I saw this red fish, I was greatly terrified and I was soon faint, but I remembered that we had sold our 'death' and I could not die again, so I did not care about it again, but I feared it greatly because we did not sell our 'fear'. At the same time that the red fish appeared out, its head was just like a tortoise's head, but it was as big as an elephant's head and it had over 30 horns and large eyes which surrounded the head. All these horns were spread out as an umbrella. It could not walk but was only gliding on the ground like a snake and its body was just like a bat's body and covered with long red hair like strings. It could only fly to a short distance, and if it shouted a person who was four miles away would hear.

All the eyes which surrounded its head were closing and opening at the same time as if a man was pressing a switch on and off.

At the same time that this red-fish saw me stood before their hole, it was laughing and coming towards me like a human-being, but I said within myself that this was a really human-being. Then I got ready as it was coming laughing towards me, but when it still had about twenty feet to reach where I stood, then I fired at it on the centre of its head and before the smoke of the gun scattered away, I had loaded again and shot it once more, so it died at that same spot. But when my wife saw the red fish when coming out from the hole, from the place where she hid herself, she ran back to the town. As the red fish was coming out from the hole, I knew that I should kill it, but I had no juju any more, all had become powerless from long using.

After that I loaded the gun for the second red creature (red-bird) and within 5 minutes it appeared out again, then I got ready for it. I saw that it was a red-bird, but its head could weigh one ton or more and it had six long teeth of about half a foot long and very thick, which appeared out with its beak. Its head was almost covered with all kinds of insects so that I could hardly describe it here fully. So immediately this bird saw me, it opened its mouth and was coming to swallow me, but I had got ready then, and when it had nearly reached the place that I stood, it stopped and swallowed the red-fish which I had killed already the first time. After that it was coming directly and I fired at it, then I loaded the gun for the second time and shot it to death.

When I saw that I had killed these two red creatures, then I remembered what my wife had said immediately we met the Red-lady who took us to the Red-king. My wife said thus:—It would be a 'fear' of heart, but it would not be dangerous to the heart."

Now I went to the Red-king of the Red-town and told him that I had killed both red creatures, and as soon as he heard so from me, he got up from his chair and followed me to the place where I killed the two red creatures. But when the Red-king saw the two red creatures already dead, he said—"Here is another fearful and harmful creature who could ruin my town in future." (He called me a fearful and harmful creature.) At the same time that he said this, he left me there and went back to the town, then he called all the people of his town together and told them what he had seen. As these Red-people could change themselves to anything that they liked, before I could reach the town, the whole of them had changed into a great fire which burnt their houses and all their properties. By the time that the houses were burning, I could not enter the town, because of the thick smoke of the fire, but after a little time the fire and smoke disappeared and I thought that the whole of them together with my wife had burnt into ashes. But as I stood in one place looking at the empty town, there I saw that two red trees appeared again at the centre of the town. One of the trees was shorter than the second and also slender and it was at the front of the bigger one. That bigger one which was at the back had many leaves and branches. When I saw that these two red trees appeared in the centre of the town I was going to them, but both were moving towards the west of the town before I reached there, and all the leaves on these trees were singing as human-beings as they were moving on and within five minutes, I could not see them any more, and all the while I did not know that it was the whole Red-people who had changed themselves into that two red trees. As my wife had disappeared with these Red-people, I began to seek her about both night and day, but one day, I heard information that she was among the Red-people who had changed themselves into two red trees before they left the Red-town. Then I started to the place where I heard that they had settled down, but the new town that they had just settled down in was about eighty miles away from the Red-town which they left ruined. After I had travelled for two days, then I reached there, but they had left there when they heard information that I was coming there too, and I did not know that these Red-people were thinking while running away from me that I should kill them as I had killed the two red creatures. So they left that place again and were looking for a suitable place to settle down, but they never got to such a place before I met them, although I was thinking that I would meet them in the form of persons, but they were the two red trees.

As I met them in the midway, my wife had seen me and was calling me, but I did not see her at all, and as I was still following these two red trees to wherever they could get a suitable place to settle down for a week. Then they got a suitable place and they stopped, but I was very far away by that time. And when I came up with them I saw that every part was full of houses, people and their domestic animals etc., exactly as when they were in the town which they had burnt into ashes before they left there. But when I entered the new town, I went directly to the Red-king of this new town (the same king) and told him that I wanted my wife, but when he heard so, he called her for me at once and she saw me, she repeated her words again which she had said before—"This would be a brief loss of woman and a shorter separation from lover," and she said that this was the meaning of the words. Then I believed her. But when the Red-people had settled down in a new town, they were no longer red, because I had killed the two red creatures which had changed them like that.

My wife had said of the woman we met: "She was not a human-being and she was not a spirit, but what was she?" She was the Red-smaller-tree who was at the front of the bigger Red-tree, and the bigger Red-tree was the Red-king of the Red-people of Red-town and the Red-bush and also the Red-leaves on the bigger Red-tree were the Red-people of the Red-town in the Red-bush".

Now my wife and I became friends with these people and we were living with them in that new town. After some days, the lady who brought us to the former town (Red-town) gave us a big house in which we were living comfortably. "She was not a human-being and she was not a spirit but what was she?" She was also the "Dance" (the lady that brought us to the Red-town) and you will remember when I mentioned the tree fellows, namely:— "DRUM, SONG AND DANCE." So when this lady (Dance) saw that I helped them greatly and they were also in a comfortable place and were no longer red, she sent for the other two fellows (Drum and Song) to come to their new town for a special occasion. But how could we enjoy these three fellows? Because nobody could beat drum as "Drum" could beat himself, nobody could sing as "Song" could sing himself, and nobody could dance as "Dance" could dance herself in this world. Who would challenge them? Nobody at all. But when the day that they appointed for this special occasion was reached, these fellows came and when "Drum" started to beat himself, all the people who had been dead for hundreds of years, rose up and came to witness "Drum" when beating; and when "Song" began to sing all domestic animals of that new town, bush animals with snakes etc, came out to see "Song" personally, but when "Dance" (that lady) started to dance the whole bush creatures, spirits, mountain creatures and also all the river creatures came to the town to see who was dancing. When these three fellows started at the same time, the whole people of the new town, the whole people that rose up from the grave, animals, snakes, spirits and other nameless creatures, were dancing together with these three fellows and it was that day that I saw that snakes were dancing more than human-beings or other creatures. When the whole people of that town and bush creatures started dancing together none of them could stop for two days. But at last "Drum" was beating himself till he reached heaven before he knew that he was out of the world and since that day he could not come to the world again. Then "Song" sang until he entered into a large river unexpectedly and we could not see him any more and "Dance" was dancing till she became a mountain and did not appear to anybody since that day, so all the deads rose up from the grave returned to the grave and since that day they could not rise up again, then all the rest of the creatures went back to the bush etc. but since that day they could not come to the town and dance with anybody or with human-beings.

So when these three fellows (Drum, Song and Dance) disappeared, the people of the new town went back to their houses. Since that day nobody could see the three fellows personally, but we are only hearing their names about in the world and nobody could do in these days what they did. After I had spent a year with my wife in this new town, I became a rich man. Then I hired many labourers to clear bush for me and it was cleared up to three miles square by these farm-labourers, then I planted the seeds and grains which were given me in the "Wraith-Island" by a certain animal (as he was called) the owner of the land on which I planted my crops, before he gave me the seeds and grains which germinated the same day as I planted them. As the seeds and grains grew up and yielded fruits the same day, so it made me richer than the rest of the people in that town.

"THE INVISIBLE-PAWN"

One night, at about ten o'clock, I saw a certain man who came to my house. He told me that he was always hearing the word—"POOR," but he did not know it and he wanted to know it. He said that he wanted to borrow some amount and he would be working for me in return as a "pawn" or as permanent hired labourer.

But when he said this, I asked how much did he want to borrow? He said that he wanted to borrow two thousand cowries (COWRIES), which was equivalent to six-pence (6d) in British money. Then I asked from my wife whether I should lend him the amount, but my wife said that the man would be a—"WONDERFUL HARD WORKER, BUT HE WOULD BE A WONDERFUL ROBBER IN FUTURE."—Of course, I did not understand what my wife meant by that, but I simply gave the man the six-pence that he demanded. When he wanted to go, I asked for his name, then he told me that his name was "GIVE AND TAKE", after that I asked him where he was living, and he replied that he was inside a bush which nobody could trace. When he said so, I asked him again, how could the other labourers reach him whenever they were going to the farm, then he replied that if the rest of the labourers were going to the farm very early in the morning, they should call his name out as they reached a junction of roads on the way to the farm. Then he went away. But when my labourers were going to the farm early in the morning, when they reached the junction and called his name out as he said (with loud voice), he answered with song. After that he asked them what kind of work they were going to do that day. Then they told him that it was only to till the ground, after that, he told them to go and till their own ground, but he would go and till his own at night, because small children must not see him and it was forbidden for adults to look at him. Then the rest of the labourers

86

went to the farm and tilled their portion. When it was early on the following morning, the rest of the labourers went to the farm as usual, but they saw the whole farm and bushes around there cleared as from a mile to fifty by this Invisible-Pawn and he had cleared all the farms which belonged to my neighbours too. So when the other labourers were going to the farm early in the morning as usual, I told them that they should tell "Invisible-Pawn" that today's work was to cut fire wood from the farm to my house. When the rest of the labourers reached there they called him and told him that today's work was to cut fire wood from the farm to the house. Then he told them to go and cut their own, and he would cut and bring his own to the house at night. As the rest of the labourers were calling him at the junction, he was not visible to them at all. But to my surprise, when everybody woke up early in the morning, we could not come out from our houses, because this man (Invisible-Pawn) had brought both fire wood and logs of wood together with palm-trees and other trees to the town, and all the town was almost covered with this wood, so that nobody could move about in the town and we did not know the time he brought them. Then all of the town's people began to clear the woods with axes etc., but it took a week before we could clear away the wood from the town. As I wanted to see him (Invisible-Pawn or Give and Take) and how he was working I told the rest farm labourers to tell "Give and Take" that today's work was to be barber for my children at home, but he told his colleagues that they should go and barb their own, he would come and barb his own at night, so the

87

rest of the labourers went away. When it was night, I told the rest of the labourers to keep watch on him and see how he would barb heads for my children, but to my surprise, it was not yet 8 o'clock in the night before everybody slept in that town, even no domestic animal was awake. After that the "Invisible-Pawn" came and barbed for all of the people in that town, adults or females with domestic animals, he took everybody to the outside before he shaved their heads, then he painted the heads with white paint, then he went back to his bush and nobody woke up till he had completed that evil work. When it was early in the morning, everybody met himself or herself outside, and when we touched our heads, they were shaven and painted with white paint. But at the same time that this new town's people woke up and saw that all the hair on the heads of their domestic animals had been cleared as well, then they rose up in alarm that they had fallen into another terrible creature's hand again. But I checked them and explained how the matter went, so by that time, they wanted me to leave their town, but I thought that I should do something to please these people, so that they would not drive me away from the town. One day, when the labourers were going to the farm, I told them to tell "Invisible-Pawn" that today's work was to go and kill bush animals and bring them to my house. When he heard so, he told them as usual. But when the day broke, the town was full of bush animals, so that all the people n the town were now pleased and did not want me to leave there again.

After that, one day, I sat down and I began to think

over how this man was working like this and he did not ask for food etc., so when the corn was ripe then I told the labourers to tell him that if he went to the farm, he should take some yams, corn etc. So they told him this when they reached the usual junction.

I did not know that this "Invisible-Pawn" or "Give and Take" was the head of all the Bush-creatures and he was the most powerful in the world of the Bush-creatures, all of these Bush-creatures were under him and working for him every night. So after he had finished that night's work in my farm together with his followers, then the whole of them took all the yams and corn etc. of my farm and took the all the yams and corn etc. from my neighbour's also. I did not know that he had followers at all who were working for him and instead of him alone taking some yams and corn, so all of them took the whole lot away at night.

Then I remembered what my wife foresaid that— "This man would be a wonderful hard worker, but he would be a wonderful robber in future." So the following morning when the labourers had told him to take some yams and corn from the farm, everybody went to his farm, but unfortunately they found their farms without crops that they had planted there, for all the farms had been cleared by these bush-creatures as flat as a football field.

But when all the farmers or my neighbours saw what "Give and Take" had done, they grew annoyed with me, because they could not plant other crops throughout that year again and had nothing for themselves and their children to eat at all and all of my own crops were taken away too, but I could not tell my neighbours. When these people saw what "Invisible-Pawn" or Give and Take" with his followers had done for them, then they united together to raise up an Army against me, so that I might leave their town and also to revenge for the great loss which "Give and Take" had given them through me. Then these people gathered together and formed a great army. Then I asked my wife what should be the end of us in this town? But my wife said that it would be the loss of lives of the natives, but it would save the two non-natives. By that time, I was hiding my wife and myself in that town, because all the natives of the town were hunting for us up and down, of course they did not want to fire guns inside their town, because of their children and wives and we (my wife and I) did not leave their town because they could not fire their guns inside the town. But as I·was thinking how my wife and myself could be safe from these people, so my wife remembered me to call for the help of the "Invisible-Pawn" (Give and Take), perhaps he might render his help. When my wife advised me like that, then I sent for one of my labourers to go and tell the "Invisible-Pawn" that the people of new town would raise up an Army against me in two days to come, so that I begged him to come and help me early in the morning of that day.

"THE INVISIBLE-PAWN ON THE FRONT"

But as the "Invisible-Pawn" could not do anything in the day time, he came with his followers or helpers to this town at about two o'clock in the mid-night, then the whole of them started to fight these people and killed the whole of them and left my wife and me there alone. As my wife had said before, all the lives of the natives were lost and the life of the non-natives saved. After that the "Invisible-Pawn" and his followers went back to their bush before dawn. But when I saw that we alone (my wife and me) could not live in that town, then we packed our loads and my gun with my cutlass and left the town as soon as all of the natives of the town had perished.

That was how our life went in the Red-town with the Red-people and the Red-king and how we saw the end of them in their new town.

So we started our journey to unknown Deads' Town, where my palm-wine tapster who had died in my town long ago was and we were travelling inside bush to bush as before, but the bush in which we were travelling by that time was not so thick and was not so fearful too. But as we were going on, my wife told me that we should not stop in there two days and nights before we should reach the place that we met the Red-lady that we followed to the Red-town and before we could reach that place, we should travel about fifty-five miles. But when we had travelled both day and night for two days, we reached there and stopped and rested there for two days. After that we started our journey to an unknown town directly, and after we had travelled ninety miles to that place, there we met a man who sat down and had a full-bag of load on his front. We asked him where was Deads' Town, and he told us that he knew, and it was the very town that he was going to at present. When he told us so, then we told him that we should follow him to the town, but when he heard so from us, he begged us to help him to carry his load which was on his front. Of course, we did not know what was inside the bag, but the bag was full, and he told us that we should not put the load down from head until we should reach the said town. Again he did not allow us to test the weight of it, whether it was heavier than what we could carry. Then my wife asked him how could a man buy a pig in a bag? But the man replied that there was no need of testing the load, he said that once we put it on our head either it was heavier than what we could carry or not, anyhow we should carry it to the town. So we stood before that man and his load. But when I thought over that if I put it on my head and could not carry it, then I should put it down at once, and if that man would force me not to put it down, I had gun and cutlass here, I should shoot him immediately.

Then I told the man to put it on my head, but he said that two hands must not touch the load. When he said so, I asked him what kind of load was this? He replied that it was the load which two persons must not know the content of. So, I put hope on my gun and I trusted my cutlass as God, then I told my wife to put the load on my head and she helped me. When I put it on my head it was just like a dead body of a man, it was very heavy, but I could carry it easily. So the man was on our front and we followed him.

But after we had travelled about 36 miles, we entered into a town and we did not know that he was telling us a lie in saying that he was going to Deads' Town and we did not know that the load was the dead body of the prince of the town that we entered. That man had mistakenly killed him in the farm and was looking for somebody who would represent him as the killer of the prince.

WE AND THE WISE KING IN THE WRONG TOWN WITH THE PRINCE KILLER

Because he (the killer of the Prince) knew that if the king realised who killed his son he (king) would kill the man instead, so this man did not want to prove out that he was the killer of the prince. So when we reached the town with him, (not Deads' Town) he told us to wait for him in a corner and he went to the king and reported to him (king) that somebody had killed his son in the bush and he had brought them to the town. Then the king sent about thirty of his attendants with the man who killed the prince to come and escort us to him with the load. When we reached the palace, they loosened the bag and saw it was the dead body of the king's son (prince), but when the king saw that it was his son, then he told his attendants to put us inside a dark room.

Early in the morning, the king told the attendants to wash and dress us with the finest clothes and put us on horse and they (attendants) must take us around the town for seven days which meant to enjoy our last life in the world for that 7 days, after that he (king) should kill us as we killed his son.

But these attendants and the right man who killed the

prince in the bush did not know the king's aim at all. When it was early in the morning, the attendants washed us and dressed us with costly clothes and dressed the horse as well. Then we mounted the horse. After that they were following us about in the town, they were beating drums, dancing and singing the song of mourning for six days, but when it was early on the 7th day's morning that we should be killed and they (attendants) were taking us around the town for the last time, we reached the centre of the town, and there we saw the right man who killed the prince and told us to carry him (prince) to that town. He pushed us away from the horse's back and mounted the horse for himself, and he told the attendants that he was the right man who killed the king's son in the bush, he said that he was thinking that the king would kill him as a revenge and that was the reason why he told the king that it was us who killed the prince in the bush. This man thought now that the king was pleased that somebody killed his son in the farm and that was the reason why the king told the attendants to dress us and take us on a riding horse about in the town, and he told the attendants again to take him to the king and repeat the same words in his presence.

So he was taken to the king and he repeated that he was the right man who killed his son in the bush. At the same time that the king heard so from him, he told the attendants to dress him as they had dressed us, then the man mounted the horse, and riding it about in the town as we had done, as he was on the horse's back, he was jumping up and laughing with gladness. When it was 5 o'clock in the evening, he was taken to their bush reserved for such occasion and he was killed there and they presented his dead body to their gods in that reserve-bush.

After we had spent 15 days in that town, then we told the king that we wanted to continue our journey to the Deads' Town, and he gave us presents and told us the shortest way to the Deads' Town. A full loaded bag would cause seven days' dance, but there would be a "WISE-KING" in the town, as my wife had foresaid. This was the end of the story of the bag which I carried from the bush to the "wrong town".

Then we continued our journey as usual to the Deads' Town and when we had travelled for 10 days we were looking at the Deads' Town about 40 miles away and we were not delayed by anything on the way again. But as we were looking at the town from a long distance, we thought that we could reach there the same day, but not at all, we travelled for 6 more days, because as we nearly reached there, it would still seem to be very far away to us or as if it was running away from us. We did not know that anybody who had not died could not enter into that town by day time, but when my wife knew the secret, then she told me that we should stop and rest till night. When it was night, then she told me to get up and start our journey again. But soon after we started to go, we found that we need not travel more than one hour before we reached there. Of course we did not enter into it until the dawn, because it was an unknown town to us.

I AND MY PALM-WINE TAPSTER
IN THE DEADS' TOWN

When it was 8 o'clock in the morning, then we entered the town and asked for my palm-wine tapster whom I was looking for from my town when he died, but the deads asked for his name and I told him that he was called "BAITY" before he died, but now I could not definitely know his present name as he had died.

When I told them his name and said that he had died in my town, they did not say anything but stayed looking at us. When it was about five minutes that they were looking at us like that, one of them asked us from where did we come? I replied that we were coming from my town, then he said where. I told him that it was very far away to this town and he asked again were the people in that town alives or deads? I replied that the whole of us in that town had never died. When he heard that from me, he told us to go back to my town where there were only alives living, he said that it was forbidden for alives to come to the Deads' Town.

As that dead man told us to go back, I began to beg him to allow us to see my palm-wine tapster. So he agreed and showed us a house which was not so far from the place where we stood, he told us to go there and ask for him, but as we turned our back to him (dead man) and were going to the house that he showed us, the whole of them that stood on that place grew annoyed at the same time to see us walking forward or with our face, because they were not walking forward there at all, but this we did not know.

As soon as the dead man who was asking us questions saw us moving he ran to us and said that he had told us to go back to my town because alives could not come and visit any dead man in the Deads' Town, so he told us to walk backward or with our back and we did so. But as we were walking backward as they themselves were walking there, I stumbled over suddenly and as I was trying not to fall into a deep pit which was near there, I mistakenly turned my face towards the house that he showed us. But when he saw me again like that, he came to us as before and said that he would not allow us to go to the house any more, because people were not walking forward in that town. Then I begged him again and explained to him that we came to see him (palm-wine tapster) from a very far town. But I stumbled on a sharp stone in that pit, some part of me was scratched and bleeding, then we stopped to rub off the blood as it was bleeding too much. When this dead man saw that we stopped, he came nearer and asked what stopped us, then I pointed my finger to the bleeding part of my body, but when he saw the blood, he was greatly annoyed and dragged us out of the town by force. As he was dragging us out of the town, we wanted to beg him, but he said, no more excuse. We did not know that all the deads did not like to see blood at all, and it was that day I knew. He dragged us out of their town and told us to stay there and we did as he said. Then he went back to the house of my tapster and told him that two alives were waiting for him. After a few minutes, my palm-wine tapster came, but immediately he saw us, he thought that I had died before coming there, so he gave the sign of deads to us, but we were unable to reply to him, because we never died, and at the same time that he reached us, he knew that we could not live with them in the town as we could not reply to his signal, then before we started any conversation, he built a small house there for us. After that we put our loads inside the house, but to my surprise, this my tapster was also walking backward and he was not walking like that before he died in my town. After he had built the house, he went back to the town and brought food and ten kegs of palm-wine for us. As we were very hungry before reaching there, we ate the food to excess and when I tasted the palm-wine, I could not take my mouth away until I drank the whole ten kegs. After that we started conversation which went thus—I told him that after he had died, I wanted to die with him and follow him to this Deads' Town because of the palm-wine that he was tapping for me and nobody could tap it for me like him, but I could not die. So one day, I called two of my friends and went to the farm, then we began to tap for ourselves, but it did not taste like the wine he was tapping before he died. But when all my friends saw that if they come to my house there was no more palm-wine to drink again, then they were leaving me one by one until all of them went away, even if I should see one of them at outside and call him, he would only say that he would come, but I would not see him come.

Though my father's house was full of people before, nobody at present was coming there. So one day, I thought what I could do, then I thought within myself that I should find him (palm-wine tapster) wherever he might be and tell him to follow me to my father's town and begin to tap palm-wine for me as usual. So I started my journey early in the morning, and at every town or village that I reached I asked them whether they had seen him or knew where he was, but some would say unless I should help them to do something, they would not tell. Then I showed the tapster my wife and told of how, when I went to a certain town and her father who was the head of that town received me as his guest, my wife was taken to a far forest by a gentleman who afterwards was reduced to a 'Skull' and how I went there and brought her to her father, so after he had seen the wonderful work which I did for him, then he gave her to me as a wife and after I had spent about one and half or more years with them there, then I took her and sought him about. And how before reaching here, we met much difficulty in the bush, because there was no road to this Deads' Town and we were travelling from bush to bush every day and night, even many times, we were travelling from branches to branches of trees for many days before touching ground and it was ten years since I had left my town. Now I was exceedingly glad to meet him here and I should be most grateful if he would follow me back to my town.

So after I had related how the story went to him, he did not talk a single word, but he went back to the town, and after a while, he brought about twenty kegs of palm-wine for me, then I started to drink it. After that he started his own story:—He said that after he had died in my town, he went to a certain place, which anybody who just died must go to first, because a person who just

99

died could not come here (Deads' Town) directly. He said that when he reached there, he spent two years in training and after he had qualified as a full dead man, then he came to this Deads' Town and was living with deads and he said that he could not say what happened to him before he died in my town. But when he said so, I told him that he fell down from a palm-tree on a Sunday evening when he was tapping palm-wine and we buried him at the foot of the very palm-tree on which he fell.

Then he said that if that should be the case, he over-drank on that day.

After that, he said that he came back to my house on the very night that he fell and died at the farm and looked at everyone of us, but we did not see him, and he was talking to us, but we did not answer, then he went away. He told us that both white and black deads were living in the Deads' Town, not a single alive was there at all. Because everything that they were doing there was in-correct to alives and everything that all alives were doing was incorrect to deads too.

He said that did I not see that both dead persons and their domestic animals of this town were walking back-wards? Then I answered "Yes." Then he told me that he could not follow me back to my town again, because a dead man could not live with alives and their charac-teristics would not be the same and said that he would give me anything that I liked in the Deads' Town. When he said so, I thought over what had happened to us in the bush, then I was very sorry for my wife and myself and I was then unable to drink the palm-wine which he gave me at that moment. Even I myself knew already that deads could not live with alives, because I had watched their doings and they did not correspond with ours at all. When it was five o'clock in the evening, he went to his house and brought food for us again and he went back after three hours. But when he came back early in the morning, he brought another 50 kegs of palm-wine which I drank first of all that morning. But when I thought that he would not follow us to my town, and again, my wife was pressing me too much to leave there very early, when he came, I told him that we should leave here tomorrow morning, then he gave me an 'EGG'. He told me to keep it as safely as gold and said that if I reached my town, I should keep it inside my box and said that the use of the egg was to give me anything that I wanted in this world and if I wanted to use it, I must put it in a big bowl of water, then I would mention the name of anything that I wanted. After he gave me the egg we left there on the third day after we arrived there and he showed us another shorter road and it was a really road, not a bush as before.

Now we started our journey from the Deads' Town directly to my home town which I had left for many years. As we were going on this road, we met over a thousand deads who were just going to the Deads' Town and if they saw us coming towards them on that road, they would branch into the bush and come back to the road at our back. Whenever they saw us, they would be making bad noise which showed us that they hated us and also were very annoyed to see alives. These deads were not talking to one another at all, even they were not talking plain words except murmuring. They always seemed as if they were mourning, their eyes would be very wild and brown and everyone of them wore white clothes without a single stain.

NONE OF THE DEADS TOO YOUNG TO ASSAULT. DEAD-BABIES ON THE ROAD-MARCH TO THE DEADS' TOWN

We met about 400 dead babies on that road who were singing the song of mourning and marching to Deads' Town at about two o'clock in the mid-night and marching towards the town like soldiers, but these dead babies did not branch into the bush as the adult-deads were doing if they met us, all of them held sticks in their hands. But when we saw that these dead babies did not care to branch for us then we stopped at the side for them to pass peacefully, but instead of that, they started to beat us with the sticks in their hands, then we began to run away inside the bush from these babies, although we did not care about any risk of that bush which might happen to us at night, because these dead babies were the most fearful creatures for us. But as we were running inside the bush very far off that road, they were still chasing us until we met a very huge man who had hung a very large bag on his shoulder and at the same time that he met us, he caught us (my wife and myself) inside the bag as a fisherman catches fishes inside his net. But when he caught us inside his bag, then all of the dead babies went back to the road and went away. As that man caught us with that bag, we met inside it many other creatures there which I could not describe here yet, so he was taking us far away into the bush. We tried with all our power to come out of the bag, but we could not do it, because it was woven with strong and thick ropes, its size was about 150 feet diameter and it could contain 45 persons. He put the bag on his shoulder as he was going and we did not know where he was taking us to by that night and again we did not know who was taking us away, whether he was a human-being or spirit or if he was going to kill us, we never knew yet at all.

AFRAID OF TOUCHING TERRIBLE CREATURES IN BAG

We were afraid of touching the other creatures that we met inside that bag, because every part of their bodies was as cold as ice and hairy and sharp as sand-paper. The air of their noses and mouths was hot as steam, none of them talked inside the bag. But as that man was carrying us away inside the bush with the bag on his shoulder the bag was always striking trees and ground but he did not care or stop, and he himself did not talk too. As he was carrying us far away into that bush, he met a creature of his kind, then he stopped and they began to throw the bag to and fro and they would take it up again and continue. After a while they stopped that, then he kept going as before, but he travelled as far as 30 miles from that road before daybreak.

HARD TO SALUTE EACH OTHER, HARDER TO DESCRIBE EACH OTHER, AND HARDEST TO LOOK AT EACH OTHER AT DESTINATION

Hard to salute each other, harder to describe each other, and hardest to look at each other at our destination. When it was 8 o'clock in the morning, this huge creature stopped when he reached his destination, and turned upside-down the bag and the whole of us in the bag came down unexpectedly. It was in that place that we saw that there were 9 terrible creatures in that bag before he caught us. Then we saw each other when we came down, but the nine terrible creatures were the hardest creatures for us to look at, then we saw the huge creature who was carrying us about in the bush throughout that night, he was just like a giant, very huge and tall, his head resembled a big pot of about ten feet in diameter, there were two large eyes on his forehead which were as big as bowls and his eyes would be turning whenever he was looking at somebody. He could see a pin at a distance of about three miles. His both feet were very long and thick as a pillar of a house, but no shoes could size his feet in this world. The description of the 9 terrible creatures in the bag is as follows. These 9 terrible creatures were short or 3 feet high, their skin as sharp as sand-paper with small short horns on their palms, very hot steam was rushing out of their noses and mouths whenever breathing, their bodies were as cold as ice and we did not understand their language, because it was sounding as a church bell. Their hands were thick about 5 inches and very short, with fingers, and also

104

their feet were just like blocks. They had no shape at all like human-beings or like other bush-creatures that we met in the past, their heads were covered with a kind of hair like sponge. Though they were very smart while walking, of course their feet would be sounding on either hard or soft ground as if somebody was walking over or knocking a covered deep hole. But immediately we came down with them from the bag and when my wife and I myself saw these terrible creatures, we closed our eyes, because of their terrible and fearful appearance. After a while, the huge creature carried us to another place, opened a rise-up hill which was in that place, he told the whole of us to enter it, then he followed us and closed the hole back, we not knowing that he would not kill us but he had only captured us as slaves. When we entered the hole, there we met other more fearful creatures who I could not describe here. So when it was early in the morning, he took us out of the hole and showed us his farm to clear as the other more fearful creatures we met in the hole were doing. As I was working with these nine creatures in the farm, one day, one of them abused me with their language which I did not under-stand, then we started to fight, but when the rest saw that I wanted to kill him, then the whole of them started to fight me one by one. I killed the first one who faced me, then the second came and I killed him too, so I killed all of them one by one until the last one came who was their champion. When I started to fight him, he began to scrape my body with his sand-paper body and also with small thorns on his palms, so that every part of my body was bleeding. But I tried with all my power to knock

105

him down and I was unable to as I could not grip him firmly with my hands, so he knocked me down and I fainted. Of course, I could not die because we had sold our death away. I did not know that my wife hid herself behind a big tree which was near the farm and that she was looking at us as we were fighting.

As there remained only the champion of the nine terrible creatures, when he saw that I had fainted, he went to a kind of plant and cut 8 leaves on it. But my wife was looking at him by that time. Then he came back to his people. After that, he squeezed the leaves with both his palms until water came out, then he began to put the water into the eyes of his people one by one and the whole of them woke up at once and all of them went to our boss (the huge creature who brought us to that place) to report what had happened in the farm to him. But at the same time that they left the farm, my wife went to that plant and cut one leaf and did as the champion did to his people, and when she pressed the water in that leaf to my eyes, then I woke up at once. As she had managed to take our loads before she left that hole and followed us to the farm, we escaped from that farm and before the nine terrible creatures reached the hole of our boss, we had gone far away. That was how we were saved from the huge creature who caught us in his bag.

As we had escaped, we were travelling both day and night so that the huge creature might not re-capture us again. When we travelled for two and half days, we reached the Deads' road from which dead babies drove us, and when we reached there, we could not travel on it because of fearful dead babies, etc. which were still on it.

106

"TO TRAVEL IN THE BUSH WAS MORE DANGEROUS AND TO TRAVEL ON THE DEADS' ROAD WAS THE MOST DANGEROUS"

Then we began to travel inside the bush, but closely to the road, so that we might not be lost in the bush again.

When we had travelled for two weeks, I began to see the leaves which were suitable for the preparation of my juju, then we stopped and prepared four kinds which could save us whenever and wherever we met any dangerous creature.

As I had prepared the juju, we did not fear anything which might happen to us inside the bush and we were travelling both day and night as we liked. So one night, we met a "hungry-creature" who was always crying "hungry" and as soon as that he saw us, he was coming to us directly. When he was about five feet away from us, we stopped and looked at him, because I had got some juju in hand already and because I remembered that we had sold our death before entering inside the white tree of the Faithful-Mother, and so I did not care about approaching him. But as he was coming towards us, he was asking us repeatedly whether we had anything for him to eat and by that time we had only bananas which were not ripe. We gave him the bananas but he swallowed all at the same moment and began to ask for another thing to eat again and he did not stop crying "hungry-hungry-hungry" once, but when we could not bear his crying, then we loosened our loads. Perhaps we could get another edible thing there to give him, but we found only a spilt bean and before we gave it to him, he had taken it from us and swallowed it without hesitation and began to cry "hungry-hungry-hungry" as usual. We did not know that this "hungry-creature" could not satisfy with any food in this world, and he might eat the whole food in this world, but he would be still feeling hungry as if he had not tasted anything for a year. But as we were searching our loads, as perhaps we could get something for him again, the egg which my tapster gave me in the Deads' Town fell down from my wife. The hungry-creature saw it, and he wanted to take it and swallow but my wife was very clever to pick it up before him.

When he saw that he could not pick it up before my wife, then he began to fight her and he said that he wanted to swallow her. As this hungry-creature was fighting with my wife, he did not stop to cry "hungry" once. But when I thought within myself that he might harm us, then I performed one of my jujus and it changed my wife and our loads to a wooden-doll and I put it in my pocket. But when the hungry-creature saw my wife no more, he told me to bring out the wooden-doll for identification, so I brought it and he was asking me with doubtful mind, was this not my wife and loads? Then I replied that it was not my wife etc., but it only resembled her, so he gave the wooden-doll back to me, then I returned it to my pocket as before and I kept going. But he was following me as I was going on, and still crying "hungry". Of course, I did not listen to him. When he had travelled with me to a distance of about a mile, he asked me again to bring out the wooden-doll for more identification and I brought it out to him, then he looked at it for more than ten minutes and asked me again was this not my wife? I replied that it was not my wife etc. but it only resembled her, then he gave it to me back and I was going as usual, but he was still following me and crying "hungry" as well. When he had travelled with me again to about two miles, he asked for it for the third time and I gave it to him, but as he held it he looked at it more than an hour and said that this was my wife and he swallowed it unexpectedly. As he swallowed the wooden-doll, it meant he swallowed my wife, gun, cutlass, egg and load and nothing remained with me again, except my juju.

So immediately he had swallowed the wooden-doll, he was going far away from me and crying "hungry" as well. Now the wife was lost and how to get her back from the hungry-creature's stomach? For the safety of an egg the wife was in hungry-creature's stomach. As I stood in that place and was looking at him as he was going far away, I saw him go so far from me that I could hardly see him, then I thought that my wife, who had been following me about in the bush to Deads' Town had not shrunk from any suffering, so I said that, she should not leave me like this and I would not leave her for the hungry-creature to carry away. So I followed, and when I met him I told him to vomit out the wooden-doll which he had swallowed, but he refused to vomit it out totally.

BOTH WIFE AND HUSBAND IN THE
HUNGRY-CREATURE'S STOMACH

I said that, rather than leave my wife with him, I would
die with him, so I began to fight him, but as he was not
a human-being, he swallowed me too and he was still
crying "hungry" and going away with us. As I was in
his stomach, I commanded my juju which changed the
wooden-doll back to my wife, gun, egg, cutlass and loads
at once. Then I loaded the gun and fired into his stomach,
but he walked for a few yards before he fell down, and
I loaded the gun for the second time and shot him again.
After that I began to cut his stomach with the cutlass,
then we got out from his stomach with our loads etc.
That was how we were freed from the hungry-creature,
but I could not describe him fully here, because it was
about 4 o'clock a.m. and that time was very dark too.
So we left him safely and thanked God for that.

We started our journey again to my home town after
we left the hungry-creature, but as he had carried
us far into the bush, we could not trace out our way to
the deads' road again, so we were travelling in the middle
of the bush. But when we had travelled for 9 days, we
entered a town in which we met mixed people, and before
we reached the "mixed town" my wife was seriously
ill, then we went to a man who resembled a human-
being, and he received us as strangers into his house,
then I began to treat my wife there. They had one native
court in this "mxed town" and I was always attending
the court to listen to many cases. But to my surprise,
one day I was told to judge a case which was brought to

the court by a man who had lent his friend a pound (£).

The story went thus:—There were two friends, one of these two friends was money borrower, he had no other work than to borrow and he was feeding on any money that he was borrowing. One day, he borrowed £1 from his friend. After a year his friend who lent him the money, asked him to refund the £1 to him, but the borrower said that he would not pay the £1 and said that he had never paid any debit since he was borrowing money and since he was born. When his friend who lent him the £1 heard so from him, he said nothing, but went back to his house quietly. One day, the lender heard information that there was a debit-collector who was bold enough to collect debits from anybody whatsoever. Then he (lender) went to the debit-collector and told him that somebody owed him £1 since a year, but he refused to pay it back; after the debit-collector heard so, then both of them went to the house of the borrower. When he had showed the house of the borrower to the collector, he went back to his home.

When the debit-collector asked for the £1 which he (borrower) had borrowed from his friend since a year, the debitor (borrower) replied that he never paid any of his debits since he was born, then the debit-collector said that *he* never failed to collect debits from any debitor since *he* had begun the work. The collector said furthermore that to collect debits about was his profession and he was living on it. But after the debitor heard so from the collector, he also said that his profession was to owe debits and he was living only on debits. In conclusion, both of them started to fight but, as they were fighting fiercely, a man who was passing that way at that time saw them and he came nearer; he stood behind them looking at them, because he was very interested in this fight and he did not part them. But when these two fellows had fought fiercely for one hour, the debitor who owed the £1 pulled out a jack-knife from his pocket and stabbed himself at the belly, so he fell down and died there. But when the debit-collector saw that the debitor died, he thought within himself that he had never failed to collect any debit from any debitor in this world since he had started the work and he (collector) said that if he could not collect the £1 from him (debitor) in this world, he (collector) would collect it in heaven. So he (collector) also pulled out a jack-knife from his pocket and stabbed himself as well, and he fell down and died there.

As the man who stood by and looking at them was very, very interested in that fight, he said that he wanted to see the end of the fight, so he jumped up and fell down at the same spot and died there as well so as to witness the end of the fight in heaven. So when the above statement was given in the court, I was asked to point out who was guilty, either the debit-collector, debitor, the man who stood by looking at them when fighting, or the lender?

But first of all, I was about to tell the court that the man who stood by them looking at them was guilty, because he should have asked about the matter and parted them, but when I remembered that the debitor and collector were doing their work on which both of them were living, then I could not blame the man who stood looking at them and again I could not blame the

112

collector, because he was doing his work and also the debitor himself because he was struggling for what he was living on. But the whole people in the court insisted me to point out who was guilty among them all. Of course when I had thought it over for two hours, then I adjourned the judgement for a year, and the court closed for that day.

So when the judgement was adjourned for a year, then I came back home and started to treat my wife as before, but when the judgement of the case which I adjourned remained four months, I was called again to the court to judge another case which went thus:—

There was a man who had three wives, these three wives loved him so much that they were following him (husband) to wherever he wanted to go, and the husband loved them as well. One day, this man (husband) was going to another town which was very far away, and his three wives followed him. But as they were travelling from bush to bush, this man (husband) stumbled over, he fell down unexpectedly and died at once. As these three wives loved him, the one who was the senior wife said that she must die with their husband so she died with him. Now there remained the second to the senior and the last one or third of the wives. Then the second to the senior who had died with their husband, said that she knew a 'Wizard' who was living in that area, and his work was to wake deads, she said that she would go and call him to come and wake their husband with the senior wife then the third wife said that she would be watching both dead-bodies so that wild animals might not eat them before the Wizard would come. So she

.vaited watching the dead-bodies before the arrival of the second wife with the Wizard. But before an hour, the second wife returned with the Wizard and he woke up their husband with the senior wife who died with their husband. After the husband woke up, he thanked the Wizard greatly and asked how much he would take for the wonderful work which he had done, but the Wizard said that he did not want money, but would be very much grateful if he (husband) could give him (Wizard) one of his three wives. When the husband heard that from the Wizard, he chose the senior wife who died with him for the Wizard but she (senior wife) refused totally; after that, he offered the second wife (who went and called the Wizard who woke the husband and senior wife up) to the Wizard, but she refused as well, then he chose the third wife who was watching the dead bodies of their husband and senior wife and she refused too. But when their husband saw that none of his wives wanted to follow the Wizard, then he told the Wizard to take the whole of them, so when the three wives heard so from their husband, they were fighting among themselves; unluckily, a police-man was passing by that time and he arrested them and charged them to the court. So the whole people in the court wanted me to choose one of the wives who was essential for the Wizard. But I could not choose any of these wives to the Wizard yet, because everyone of them showed her part of love to their husband in that the senior wife died with their husband, the second wife went and called the Wizard who woke the husband and senior wife and the third protected the dead bodies from the wild-animals till the second wife brought the Wizard. So I adjourned the judgement of the case for a year as well. But before the date of the two cases expired my wife was very well and we left that town (mixed town) and before I reached my home town, the people of the "mixed town" had sent more than four letters, I met the letters at home, to come and judge the two cases, because both were still pending or waiting for me.

So I shall be very much grateful if anyone who reads this story-book can judge one or both cases and send the judgement to me as early as possible, because the whole people in the "mixed town" want me very urgently to come and judge the two cases.

After we left the "mixed town", we travelled more than 15 days before we saw a mountain, then we climbed it and met more than a million mountain-creatures as I could describe them.

WE AND THE MOUNTAIN-CREATURES ON THE UNKNOWN-MOUNTAIN

When we reached the top of this mountain, we met uncountable mountain-creatures who resembled human-beings in appearance, but they were not, the top of this "Unknown-mountain" was as flat as a football field and every part of it was lighted with various colours of lights and decorated as if it was a hall, so these mountain-creatures were dancing in form of circles when we met them. But when we reached the middle of them, they stopped dancing and we stood among them and we were looking at the bush very far away from that place. As these "mountain-creatures" loved to dance always, they asked my wife to join them and she did.

TO SEE THE MOUNTAIN-CREATURES WAS NOT DANGEROUS BUT TO DANCE WITH THEM WAS THE MOST DANGEROUS

They were very pleased as my wife was dancing with them, but when my wife felt tired, these creatures were not tired, then my wife stopped, and when they saw her all of them were greatly annoyed and dragged her to continue with them and when she started again, she became tired before them, so she stopped as before, then they came to her and said that she must dance until she should be released. But as she was dancing again and when I saw that she was exceedingly tired and these creatures did not stop at all, then I went to her and said to her "let us go," but as she was following me, these creatures grew annoyed with me. They wanted to take her back to the dance from me by force. So I performed my juju there again, and it changed my wife into the wooden-doll as usual, then I put it into my pocket, and they saw her no more.

But when she had disappeared from their presence they told me to find her out at once and grew annoyed by that time, so I started to run away for my life because I could not face them to fight at all. As I was running away from them, I could not run more than 300 yards

116

before the whole of them caught me and surrounded me there; of course, before they could do anything to me, I myself had changed into a flat pebble and was throwing myself along the way to my home town.

But these "mountain-creatures" were still following me and trying their best to catch me as I was a pebble, although, they were unable to catch it until I (pebble) reached the river which crossed the road to my town and also the river was near my town. But before reaching the river, I was very tired and nearly broke into two, because of striking harder stones as I was throwing myself, but at the same time that I reached the river, they nearly caught me there. But without any ado, I threw myself to the other side of the river and before touching the ground, I had changed myself into man, and also my wife, gun, egg, cutlass and loads as usual and at the same time that we touched the ground, we bade the "mountain-creatures" good-bye and they were looking at us as we were going, because they must not cross the river at all. That was how we left the "mountain-creatures". So from that river to my home town was only a few minutes to reach. Then we entered on my father's land, and no harm or bad creatures came again.

When it was 7 o'clock early in the morning, we reached my town, then we entered my parlour, but at the same time that my town's people saw that I returned, they rushed to my house and greeted us. So both of us reached my town safely and I met my parents safely too, with all my old friends who were coming to my house and drinking palm-wine with me before I left.

After that, I sent for 200 kegs of palm-wine and drank

it together with my old friends as before I left home. Immediately I reached my home, I entered my room and opened my box, then I hid the egg which my palm-win tapster gave from the Deads' Town. And so all our trials, difficulties and many years' travel brought only an egg or resulted in an egg.

But on the third day after we arrived home, my wife and I went to her father in his town and met them also in good condition, then we returned after we had spent three days there. That was how the story of the palm-wine drinkard and his dead palm-wine tapster went

Before reaching my town, there was a great famine (FAMINE), and it killed millions of the old people and uncountable adults and children, even many parents were killing their children for food so as to save themselves after they had eaten both domestic animals and lizards etc. Every plant and tree and river dried away for lack of the rain, and nothing for the people to eat remained.

THE CAUSES OF THE FAMINE

In the olden days, both Land and Heaven were tight friends as they were once human-beings. So one day, Heaven came down from heaven to Land his friend and he told him to let them go to the bush and hunt for the bush animals; Land agreed to what Heaven told him. After that they went into a bush with their bows and arrows, but after they had reached the bush, they were hunting for animals from morning till 12 o'clock a.m., but nothing was killed in that bush, then they left that

118

bush and went to a big field and were hunting there till 5 o'clock in the evening and nothing was killed there as well. After that, they left there again to go to a forest and it was 7 o'clock before they could find a mouse and started to hunt for another, so that they might share them one by one, because the one they had killed already was too small to share, but they did not kill any more. After that they came back to a certain place with the one that they had killed and both of them were thinking how to share it. But as this mouse was too small to divide into two and these two friends were also greedy, Land said that he would take it away and Heaven said that he would take it away.

WHO WILL TAKE THE MOUSE?

But who would take the mouse? So Land refused totally for Heaven to take it and Heaven refused totally for Land to take it away and Land said that he was senior to Heaven and Heaven said that too, but when they argued for many hours, both were vexed and went away, and they left the mouse there. Heaven returned to heaven his home and Land went back to his house on the earth.

But when Heaven reached the heaven, he stopped rain falling to the earth even he did not send dew to the earth at all, and everything dried away on earth, and nothing remained for the people of the world with which to feed themselves, so both living creatures and non-livings be gan to die away.

AN EGG FED THE WHOLE WORLD

Now as there was a great famine before I arrived in my town, so I went to my room and put water into a bowl and put the egg inside it, then I commanded the egg to produce food and drinks which my wife and my parents and myself would eat, but before a second there I saw that the room had become full of varieties of food and drinks, so we ate and drank to our satisfaction. After that, I sent for all of my old friends and gave them the rest of the food and the drinks, after that, the whole of us began to dance and when they required more, then I commanded the egg again and produced many kegs and drank it, after that, my friends asked me how did I manage to gèt these things. They said for 6 years, they never tasted water and palm-wine at all, then I told them that I brought the palm-wine etc. from the Deads' Town.

And it was a late hour in the night before they went back to their houses. But to my surprise, I did not get up from my bed early in the morning before they came and woke me up and they increased by 60 per-cent, so when I saw them like that, I entered into my room where I hid the egg and opened the box, I put it in the bowl with water and commanded it as usual, so it produced both food and drinks for all of them (friends) etc., and I left them in my parlour, because they did not go in time. Now, the news of the wonderful egg was spreading from town to town and from village to village. One morning when I woke up from my bed, it was hard to open the door of my house, because all the people from various towns and villages had come and waited there to eat, even they were too numerous to count and before 9 o'clock my town could not contain strangers. So when it was ten o'clock and when the whole of these people sat down quietly, then I commanded the egg as before and at once, it produced food and drinks for each of these people, so that everyone of them who had not eaten for a year, ate and drank to his or her satisfaction, then they took the rest of the food etc. to their towns or houses. But after the whole of them had gone away temporarily, then I commanded the egg to produce a lot of money and it produced it at once, so I hid it somewhere in my room. As everyone of those people knew that whenever they come to my house they would eat and drink as he or she liked, so it would not be two o'clock in the mid-night before people would be arriving from the various towns and villages to my house and they were bringing their children and old people along with them. All the kings and their attendants came too. When I could not sleep because of their noise, then I got up from bed and I wanted to open the door, but they rushed violently into the house and damaged the door. So when I tried my best to push them back and failed, then I told them that everyone would not be served unless at outside, but after they heard so, they went back to the outside and waited at the front of my house. Then I myself got out and commanded the egg to supply them with food and drinks. Now the people were rapidly increasing from various towns or unknown places, but the worst part of it was if they came, they would not return again to their towns, so I got no chance to sleep once or to rest, except to command the egg throughout the day and night, but when I found that keeping the egg inside the room was causing much trouble for me, then I put it together with the bowl outside in the middle of these people.

RECKLESS LIFE AT HOME

As I had become the greatest man in my town and did no other work than to command the egg to produce food and drinks, so one day, when I commanded the egg to supply the best food and drinks in the world to these people, at the same time it did so, but when these people ate the food and drank to their satisfaction, they began to play and were wrestling with each other until the egg was mistakenly smashed, the egg with the bowl broken, the egg itself broken into two. Then I took it and gummed it. But these people still remained there, even they not playing etc. and sorry for the egg which broke, of course, when they were feeling hungry again, they asked for food etc. as usual. So I brought out the egg and commanded it as before, but it could not produce out anything again and I commanded it three times in their presence but nothing was produced. When these people had waited there for four days without eating and drinking anything, then they were returning to their towns etc. one by one, but they were abusing me as they were leaving.

PAY WHAT YOU OWE ME AND VOMIT
WHAT YOU ATE

After these people had gone back to where they came, nobody came to my house as before, and all my friends stopped coming too, even whenever I saw them outside and saluted them, they would not answer me at all. But I did not care for that, because I had a lot of money in my room. But as I did not throw the egg away when broken, so one day, I went to my room and re-gummed it securely, then I commanded it as perhaps it might produce food as usual. And to my surprise, it produced only millions of leather-whips, but immediately I saw what it could produce, I commanded it again to take the whips back and it did so at once. After a few days, I went to the king and told him to tell his bell ringers to ring the bell to every town and village and tell the whole people that they should come to my house and eat etc., as before, because my palm-wine tapster who gave me the first wonderful egg had sent another egg to me from the Deads' Town, and this one was even more powerful than the first one which broke.

But when these people heard so, the whole of them came and when I saw that none of them remained behind, then I put the egg in the middle of them, after that I told one of my friends to command it to produce anything it could for them, then I entered my house and closed all the windows and doors. When he commanded it to produce anything it could, the egg produced only millions of whips and started to flog them all at once, so those who brought their children and old people did not remember to take them away before they escaped. All the king's attendants were severely beaten by these whips and also all the kings. Many of them ran into the bush and many of them died there, especially old people and children and many of my friends died as well, and it was hard for the rest to find his or her way back home, and within an hour none of them remained at the front of my house.

When these whips saw that all the people had gone away, then the whole of them (whips) gathered into one place and formed an egg as before, but to my astonishment it disappeared at the same time. But the great famine was still going on seriously in every part of the town, although when I saw that many old people began to die every day, then I called the rest of the old people who remained and told them how we could stop the famine. We stopped the famine thus:—We made a sacrifice of two fowls, 6 kolas, one bottle of palm oil, and 6 bitter kolas. Then we killed the fowls and put them in a broken pot, after that we put the kolas and poured the oil in the pot. The sacrifice was to be carried to Heaven in heaven.

BUT WHO WOULD CARRY THE SACRIFICE TO THE HEAVEN FOR HEAVEN?

First we chose one of the king's attendants, but that one refused to go, then we chose one of the poorest men in the town and he refused also, at last we chose one of the king's slaves who took the sacrifice to heaven for Heaven who was senior to Land and Heaven received the sacrifice with gladness. The sacrifice meant that Land surrendered, that he was junior to Heaven. But when the slave carried the sacrifice to heaven and gave it to Heaven he (slave) could not reach halfway back to the earth before a heavy rain came and when the slave was beaten by this heavy rain and when he reached the town, he wanted to escape from the rain, but nobody would allow him to enter his or her house at all. All the people were thinking that he (slave) would carry them also to Heaven as he had carried the sacrifice to Heaven, and were afraid.

But when for three months the rain had been falling regularly, there was no famine again.

I am the native of Abeokuta, and I was born in the year 1920. Abeokuta is 64 miles to Lagos. When I was about 7 years old, one of my father's cousins whose name is Dalley, a nurse in the African hospital, took me from my father to his friend Mr. F. O. Monu, an Ibe man, to live with him as a servant and to send me to school instead of paying me money.

I started my first education at the Salvation Army School, Abeokuta, in the year 1934, and Mr. Monu was paying my school fees regularly, which were 1/6 a quarter, and also buying the school materials, etc., for me.

But as I had the quicker brain than the other boys in our class (Class I infant), I was given the special promotion from Class I to Std. I at the end of the year.

After the school hour or every Saturday, I would go to far bush to fetch for firewood, so my master did not spend money on this again.

Having spent two years with my master, he was transferred to Lagos in 1936, and I followed him through his kindness. Having reached Lagos, we were living in an upstair at Bliss St., near Ita Faji.

A few weeks after we arrived in Lagos, I was admitted into a school called Lagos High School. No, I was not the one who was preparing food, etc., for my master, but a cruel-hearted woman, so, before I could go to the school, which is about a mile, this woman would force me to grind pepper, to split wood, to wash plates and to draw sufficient water from the pump to the house before she would allow me to go to the school at about 9:30 A.M., while the school starts at

126

8:30. And she would not give me breakfast at all before I left home for school.

In the recess time or at 12 o'clock, all the rest of the boys in the classes would go out for their food but I alone would remain in the class to be studying all the subjects taught us before the recess. When we closed finally at four o'clock and I reached home, this woman would only give me a full cup of gari instead of two which could satisfy me and again she would not put meat in the soup for me.

This hard-hearted woman was serving my master to his entire satisfaction, by this trick she had the chance to save some pennies which she ought to use for me. Although I had the chance to complain to my master about this ill-treatment, I was afraid that she would drive me away from my master through bad reports, because she was very trickish and I myself did not want to break my learning.

I attended this school for a year, and my weekly report card columns were always marked 1st position on every week-end, which means I was the first boy out of 50 boys in the class throughout the year. At the end of that year I was in the list position out of 150 boys and this was the final examination of the year. For this reason, the Principal of this school promoted me from Std. II to Std. IV and he also allowed me to attend the school free of charge for one year.

But having passed from Std. IV to V the following year, I was unable to remain with my master any longer, because the severe punishments given to me at home by this woman were too much for me, so, on December holiday, I told my master that I wanted to go to Abeokuta to visit my father and mother. When I reached home, I refused to go back to Lagos again, but as my master loved me as his brother or son, he came to Abeokuta to know what delayed me.

But still I refused to follow him back to Lagos, because I remembered the cruel-hearted woman, and this is the way I broke my learning. Again, I started to attend the school at Abeokuta once more, the name of this school is Anglican Central School, Ipose Ake, Abeokuta. At this time, I was not under a master, but my father, who was living at a village a distance of 23¾ miles to Abeokuta, was paying my school fees and living. But as I was so young at that time, whenever I went to my father for my chop money and returned to the town (Abeokuta), this chop money would not last me more than 2 weeks before it was finished, because it was not sufficient for my requirements at all, then I would go around the bush that was near the town to fetch for firewood which I was selling to earn my living temporarily. On Saturday, I would go to my father if I needed something from him, but I was trekking this distance of 23¾ miles instead of joining a lorry, because I had no money to pay for transport which was then only 2d. If I left home at 6 o'clock in the morning, I would reach the village at about 8 o'clock in the same morning or when my people were just preparing to go to farm, and this was a great surprise to them, because they did not believe that I trekked the distance but joined a lorry. Having reached the village on that morning and having eaten I would follow my father to the farm to assist him till the evening.

On the following day, which is Sunday, my father would give me my chop money plus 2d for transport, then I would leave the village at about 5 o'clock in the evening to join the lorry at a distance of 5 miles from this village, as from there the transport is available to Abeokuta. But instead of joining the lorry and paying the 2d to the lorry owner I would keep it in my pocket for other purposes, and I would trek the distance to the town.

One day, when I tired of trekking this distance and I had no money with me, I joined a lorry to "stow-away" to my destination, so, this made the lorry owner suspect me that I was a "stow-away," and my forehead was wounded as a result of injuries which gave me a scar on the forehead.

At the end of that year, I passed from Std. V to VI, and after I spent nine months on Std. VI my father, who was paying the school fees, etc., died unexpectedly (1939). Now, there was none of my family who volunteered to assist me to further my studies. Then I left the school and went to the farm or village, so, I started to make my own farm, as I must not touch my father's farm or his properties, as it then belonged only to the family. As I was making this farm, my aim was that if the crops I planted produced fruit I would sell it and have some money to pay for the school fees, etc., because I wanted to complete the Std. VI, but unluckily, there were not enough rains in that year which could enable the crops to yield well. Having spent about a year at the farm unsuccessfully, I went to my brother at Lagos (we were born by the same father and not by the same mother). Then I started to learn smithery. Having qualified for this trade, I struggled and joined the W. African Air Corps (RAF) in the year 1944, as a Coppersmith, as blacksmithing also pertains to this trade. My rank is AAI, and the number is WA/8624.

Having demobilized, I tried my possible best to establish my own job, but after a few months I was unable to carry it on, because I had not sufficient money to establish the work and because I had nobody to assist me. Having failed in this, I started to go here and there for a better job. So,

129

at that time, all the overseas soldiers had come back in large numbers and all were looking for jobs; when a post was vacant, about one hundred persons would rush there. For this reason, it was hard for me before I obtained this unsatisfactory job which I am still carrying on at present.

Amos Tutuola
17.4.52.

Selected Grove Press Paperbacks

62480-7   ACKER, KATHY / Great Expectations: A Novel / $6.95

17458-5   ALLEN, DONALD & BUTTERICK, GEORGE F., eds. / The Postmoderns: The New American Poetry Revised / $9.95

7397-X   ANONYMOUS / My Secret Life / $4.95

62433-5   BARASH, D. and LIPTON, J. / Stop Nuclear War! A Handbook / $7.95

7087-3   BARNES, JOHN / Evita—First Lady: A Biography of Eva Peron / $4.95

7208-6   BECKETT, SAMUEL / Endgame / $2.95

7299-X   BECKETT, SAMUEL / Three Novels: Molloy, Malone Dies and The Unnamable / $4.95

7204-3   BECKETT, SAMUEL / Waiting for Godot / $3.50

2064-X   BECKETT, SAMUEL / Worstward Ho / $5.95

7244-2   BORGES, JORGE LUIS / Ficciones / $6.95

7112-8   BRECHT, BERTOLT / Galileo / $2.95

7106-3   BRECHT, BERTOLT / Mother Courage and Her Children / $2.45

7393-7   BRETON, ANDRE / Nadja / $5.95

7439-9   BULGAKOV, MIKHAIL / The Master and Margarita / $4.95

7108-X   BURROUGHS, WILLIAM S. / Naked Lunch / $3.95

7749-5   BURROUGHS, WILLIAM S. / The Soft Machine, Nova Express, The Wild Boys: Three Novels / $5.95

2488-2   CLARK, AL, ed. / The Film Year Book 1984 / $12.95

7535-2   COWARD, NOEL / Three Plays (Private Lives, Hay Fever, Blithe Spirit) / $4.50

7219-1   CUMMINGS, E. E. / 100 Selected Poems / $2.95

7327-9   FANON, FRANZ / The Wretched of the Earth / $4.95

7483-6   FROMM, ERICH / The Forgotten Language / $6.95

7390-2   GENET, JEAN / The Maids and Deathwatch: Two Plays / $5.95

7838-6   GENET, JEAN / Querelle / $4.95

7662-6   GERVASI, TOM / Arsenal of Democracy II / $12.95

7956-0   GETTLEMAN, MARVIN, et. al. eds. / El Salvador: Central America in the New Cold War / $9.95

7648-0   GIRODIAS, MAURICE, ed. / The Olympia Reader / $5.95

2490-4   GUITAR PLAYER MAGAZINE / The Guitar Player Book (Revised and Updated Edition) / $11.95

7003-8   HITLER, ADOLF / Hitler's Secret Book / $7.95

7125-X   HOCHHUTH, ROLF / The Deputy / $4.95

7115-8   HOLMES, BURTON / The Olympian Games in Athens, 1896 / $6.95

GROVE PRESS, INC., 196 West Houston St., New York, N.Y 10014